As always:

To my beta-readers and "feedback crew": I am so glad you are all here. And I am so glad you are all so blunt with me—even if I do what I want most of the time.

To all of the readers: It has been quite a journey. I've loved every second of it. Let's get to the end together, shall we?

Also by Chase Connor

Just a Dumb Surfer Dude: A Gay Coming-of-Age Tale
Just a Dumb Surfer Dude 2: For the Love of Logan
Just a Dumb Surfer Dude 3: Summer Hearts
Gavin's Big Gay Checklist
A Surplus of Light
The Guy Gets Teddy
GINJUH
A Tremendous Amount of Normal
The Gravity of Nothing
Between Enzo & the Universe

A Point Worth LGBTQ Paranormal Romances

Jacob Michaels Is Tired (Book 1)
Jacob Michaels Is Not Crazy (Book 2)
Jacob Michaels Is Not Jacob Michaels (Book 3)
Jacob Michaels Is Not Here (Book 4)
Jacob Michaels Is Trouble (Book 5)
CARNAVAL (A Point Worth LGBTQ Paranormal Romance Story)
Jacob Michaels Is Dead (Book 6)

Erotica

Bully

Audiobooks

A Surplus of Light: A Gay Coming-of-Age Tale

A Tremendous
Amount of Normal

"Nobody realizes that some people expend a tremendous energy merely to be normal."

~ Albert Camus

Table of Contents

Part 1

Chapter 1 – *Noah – page 3*
Chapter 2 – *Will – page 21*
Chapter 3 – *Noah – page 37*
Chapter 4 – *Will – page 51*
Chapter 5 – *Noah – page 73*
Chapter 6 – *Will – page 83*
Chapter 7 – *Manny – page 99*
Chapter 8 – *Will – page 107*

Part 2

Chapter 9 – *Will – page 127*
Chapter 10 – *Manny – page 139*
Chapter 11 – *Noah – page 149*
Chapter 12 – *Manny – page 157*
Chapter 13 – *Will – page 161*
Chapter 14 – *Will – page 173*

Part 3

Chapter 15 – *Noah – page 197*
Chapter 16 – *Will – page 205*
Chapter 17 – *Manny – page 217*
Chapter 18 – *Noah – page 227*
Chapter 19 – *Manny – page 235*
Chapter 20 – *Will – page 241*
Chapter 21 – *Noah – page 253*
Chapter 22 – *Will – page 259*
Chapter 23 – *Manny – page 269*

Part One

A Tremendous Amount of Normal

Chapter 1
Noah

Normally, I don't have a meltdown when we run out of oranges. I have some coping skills that help me deal with unexpected changes in my daily routine. That is what my doctor calls my repetitive movements. Coping Skills. Apparently, routine is important to me. A "routine" is "*a sequence of actions regularly followed; a fixed program.*" Routine is security and comfort. It lets people know that their life is static. That they will not have to deal with unforeseen obstacles throughout the day. To me, Routine is the antithesis of Anxiety. Anxiety is chaos. Routine is not.

When I saw the sliced pear on my breakfast plate, I tried touching my thumb to each of my fingers in succession. Thumb to forefinger. Thumb to middle finger. Thumb to ring finger. Thumb to little finger. Then I repeated it. Ten times. It was not working to alleviate my Anxiety. I added rocking side to side to my finger movements. Things just got faster. I was thinking more quickly than normal. I think pretty quickly normally. I think a lot normally. The chewing at my bottom lip began. In an hour I will go to school with a bloody lip and a bump on my forehead.

It happens often.

My brother has to talk to the principal on those days.

Pears feel like sand between my teeth. Like chewing white granulated sugar. But it is also wet. And the juice is not distributed evenly throughout the slice of pear. One bite may be dry and feel like sand. The next bite may feel like wet sand in my mouth. All of the bites until the last one may be dry. Then the last one is wet. The last bite shocks me. Unnerves me. Makes me start touching my fingers to my thumb.

When I saw the pear on my plate, I knew that the pear would be fine. Until the last bite. Then there would be a squirt of grainy pear juice across my tongue and lips. Shoving a whole slice of a pear into my mouth is not a solution to keeping my lips from getting sticky and grainy. I've tried. Doing that with an orange is easy, but a pear is impossible. It is too much. Too much texture. Too many rough edges. Too many uncertainties. An orange will be wet but contained to my mouth. An orange will always be soft and easily chewable. It's juicy throughout. The texture is basically the same from one orange to the next. Pears are not like that.

Pears are Chaos.

I do not like Chaos.

I like Routine.

I'm only good with Chaos if my brother is around.

Normally, when I have a meltdown—which is what my mom and my doctor call it when I am processing a lot of information at once when I am really anxious—I don't really have control over my body. Not having control is probably not the way that a person would describe what happens inside of me. Because I have a level of control. But I cannot have control over my excessive thoughts, my Anxiety, and my repetitive movements all at once at a level that is normal. I let my body become one big repetitive movement. I hope that it helps to calm my Anxiety quicker. Banging my head on the table seems to help a lot, hitting myself in the chest distracts from the excessive thoughts, sometimes scratching my skin to elicit pain is helpful.

I read once that small children have "tantrums." A "tantrum" is "*an uncontrolled outburst of anger and frustration, typically in a young child.*" I like saying the word in my head. It is a melodic and rhythmic word.

Tantrum.

Tantrum.

Tantrum.

Tantrum.

Tantrum.

Tantrum.

Tantrum.

Tantrum.

Tantrum.

Tantrum.

The word is a coping skill—a repetitive movement—that I can keep to myself so that I appear more normal. The word is like a chant. Sometimes it can also help me ease my Anxiety. But I don't have tantrums. I am not angry or frustrated when I do my repetitive movements excessively. I am anxious. I feel overwhelmed by my thoughts. Sometimes, in the right environment, if it is quiet enough, if it is dark enough, touching my fingers to my fingers in order can ease my Anxiety. It takes more than ten touches, but I don't have to rock back and forth or bang my head or scratch my skin, or hit myself in the chest.

My doctor described my meltdowns as tantrums once. I am not really sure why he used that word since it is not accurate and I assume that a doctor would want to be precise. I asked my mom after we left the doctor's office what he meant by saying that I had "tantrums," but she told me to try to forget it. I can't forget things. Telling me to forget things makes it worse. I concentrate so hard on trying to forget something that it is all that I think about. Then I get anxious. I question the thing I'm trying to forget even more.

The thing plays in my head on repeat.

Maybe for minutes.

And it won't stop.

Maybe for hours.

I still don't understand why Thomas Johnson started calling me a retard in fifth grade.

Maybe for years.

I told him that I am not a retard because my I.Q. is actually higher than average and I don't have any mental disabilities or dysfunctions and that my grades were good. His friends then called me a retard, too. One of them pushed me because he said that's what happens to retards. I know there was something I didn't understand. I don't understand people a lot. I don't understand how they use words. But my repetitive movements didn't help that day. And banging my head against the sidewalk at the bus stop didn't fix it. When my mom took me to the hospital, the doctor in the emergency room told me I could pick out either the royal blue or beige bandages to go over the stitches on my forehead and cheek. That was interesting. I picked blue. She gave me blue.

I like blue.

I like simple choices.

My mom had to talk to the principal when I went back to school.

Mom said it was because he was worried that I was being bullied.

"Bullied" means "*when one uses superior strength or influence to intimidate someone, typically to force him or her to do what one wants.*"

I didn't remember being bullied.

But I trust my mom. Mostly.

And Principal Hoffman was a really smart man.

He was probably right.

I just have my doubts.

Principal Hoffman was old and fat and breathed really deeply when he walked. When I told him he was fat, he told me that I was right but that we should only talk about it together because other people didn't like the word. His face was always red when he walked from one end of the school to the other. Whenever he was around the cafeteria ladies had toasted and untoasted bread for breakfast at school. Which made me happy, I think. I like untoasted bread because then I don't get crumbs on my shirt and stuck between my cheeks and my teeth. And there was always grape jelly without grape pieces in it when Principal Hoffman was around, too. I don't like jam. I like the purple kind of jelly. I told him once that I liked plain bread with the purple grape jelly. And Principal Hoffman told me that he liked plain bread with purple grape jelly, too. He was amazed at the coincidence that we liked the same thing so much. I really liked Principal Hoffman.

He also liked corn tortillas with just eggs and black beans and cheddar cheese when they had breakfast tacos. I told him that Brandon Waters liked corn tortillas with just eggs and black beans and cheddar cheese, too, because he had Celiac disease. Principal Hoffman thought it was amazing that he had so many food preferences in common with two different students. The next morning, he sat at the table with Brandon Waters and me and asked us what all foods we liked. It was really amazing that he liked all the same foods and told us he was going to talk to the lunch ladies and make sure that they had those foods for just the three of us. But we never got our food from the lunch ladies. Principal Hoffman always had our lunches put in paper bags for us that he kept in his fridge for us until lunch. The white paper bags that look clean. Principal Hoffman would sit with Brandon and me during lunch and eat with us and tell us how much he was still amazed that we all had such great opinions about food.

Kids wouldn't talk so loud to Brandon and me during lunch when Principal Hoffman was there because they didn't want to disturb his lunch. Which I thought was probably really nice of them. After

Brandon moved to California with his family, though, Principal Hoffman also started having to go to a lot of meetings during lunch. Without someone to focus on, I didn't enjoy lunches so much. The other kids got loud again.

Sometimes I miss having Principal Hoffman as my principal. The cafeteria at the middle school was really loud and bright. The windows let in a lot of sunlight, so I don't know why they also had all of the lights on, too. And the other kids always screamed questions at me. Luckily, Principal Hoffman started needing me to watch his office for him while he went to meetings during lunch, and he preferred that the lights stayed off while he was gone. He told me that wasting electricity is bad. He's right. He knew a lot of important things like that. Things about school that only the two of us seemed to understand. Helping him out was really nice since his office was dark and quiet and he kept the thermostat at seventy degrees. I don't like it when it's hot, and I sweat. He would even come back a few minutes before lunch was over each day and turn the lights on so that we could talk. He liked to speak quietly. I liked that. He didn't even get onto me when I cinched my hoodie tightly around my face. Luckily, by the time I had to go to class, my eyes were used to the lights so I could uncinch my hood and not get in trouble in my next class.

Everyone says Principal Hoffman had his heart attack because he was really fat. Heart disease is more common in fat people. I don't know why Principal Hoffman was really fat. I really liked having him as my principal.

The principal I have at the high school doesn't like plain bread and purple grape jelly without the grape pieces in it. Usually, there is toast and strawberry jam at breakfast in the cafeteria. I eat at home before my brother takes me to school. Normally, I eat plain bread with purple grape jelly without the grape pieces, almonds without the skins, and a glass of skim milk. I don't like two percent or whole milk. It feels thick in my mouth. It leaves a film on my tongue and my teeth. I also eat an orange. Normally.

I don't really mind too much when my brother touches me. When he grabs my head, he always puts a dishtowel in his hand first. Then his skin doesn't touch mine directly. I don't feel his rough fingerprints and the hairs on the back of his hand on my forehead. I don't mind that he holds me from behind when he does it, either because his shirt and hoodie and my shirt and hoodie keep me from feeling too much of his body. Sometimes I can feel the zipper of his hoodie against my back through all of our clothes, but it's not really too bad most of the time. And he always makes sure that he doesn't touch my torso with his hands. And only his chest touches my back so that he doesn't touch too much of my body all at once.

I like that he likes hugging people the way I like to be hugged.

I don't like being hugged much.

But I let my brother hug me.

His hugs don't make my skin itch and crawl.

And he never talks directly into my ear.

He keeps his lips away from my ear.

He turns his head to the side when he talks while hugging me.

His voice is really deep.

I can feel his chest vibrate against my back when he talks to me when he's hugging me.

It's like one of those massage chairs at the mall.

Except that I don't have to be touched all over.

I like his hugs more than any other hugs.

And I don't like most hugs.

He even rocks back and forth with me, so I usually forget that my head hasn't hit the table since he started hugging me. Sometimes he also hits his hand against my forehead through the dishtowel in the same rhythm as I do against the table. Which is nice. It's not as hard, so it's not the same, but it's nice. I like the rhythm and sound of it. He doesn't do this often, but anytime I feel overwhelmed, he hugs me, and we do repetitive movements together.

My brother will wrap his arms around me, never touching me directly with his hands, and will rock back and forth with me and hit my head softly and rhythmically so that I can keep touching my fingers to my thumb. We used to do that a lot. But this is the first time that we've hugged in forty-seven days. Sometimes I miss it, but only when I'm really anxious. I sometimes think about asking him to hug me without touching me with his hands when I get anxious, but he is busy a lot, and I don't want to bother him. So, I'll scratch myself and touch my fingers to each other instead. He gets sad when he sees my scratches and makes me promise to come and find him the next time I feel like scratching myself.

My brother is a fag. That's what my sister says. Usually when she's angry. "Fag" means "*to work hard or toil,*" or "*a tiring or unwelcome task.*" I guess she thinks he's annoying to put up with. But she also calls me a retard sometimes, so I think that maybe she doesn't really know what she means to say. That's what my brother tells me when she calls him a fag or she calls me a retard. He'll tell me that she's just confused. Sometimes he'll hug me like I like afterward. Never with his hands.

I don't think that my brother is annoying. On the weekends, when he's done writing all of his papers and finishing his projects for his college classes, he listens to music with me. He will plug his two sets of headphones into his laptop and play songs that I like at the volume that I like. We usually lay on his bed together, and he will set the laptop on his chest and beat his hands against the mattress to the rhythm of the songs. I like the vibrations his hands create on the bed. It's like being hugged without hands.

He even likes watching cartoons with the closed captions on.

I like that, too.

He even stopped making me take showers a few years ago. Now he'll let me take baths so that my hair doesn't get wet and lay against my forehead like seaweed. After I get my bath, he washes my hair in the sink, making sure it never lays on my forehead for long. He even dries it the way I like, with the blow dryer on the cool setting so that my forehead doesn't get sweaty so that when my hair lays against it, my hair doesn't feel like seaweed anyway.

He likes drying his hair that way, too. He says he would never use the blow dryer on the hot setting, so he would never make me do that either.

My brother also is really good about explaining to my mom about pears and oranges. Which is good. Because I'm not. Sometimes he does it loudly, but never while he's hugging me and never directly into my ear. When he's hugging me, he'll just remind her that I like oranges and not pears and to get some at the store when she gets off of work. By the time he's done hugging me, though, he usually just tells her to forget about it, and he'll do it himself. That is always interesting that he changes his mind so much but always hugs me the same way.

My brother used to have a friend that he would hang out with a lot. Right after he started going to college and I started my freshmen year of high school. They'd be gone all afternoon and evening, and then my brother would come home to help me get my bath and wash my hair. After two months of hanging out with his friend, he asked me if it would be okay if he hung out with his friend all night. I thought it was nice that they liked being around each other so much.

The only person that I like being around all the time is my brother.

That made sense to me.

That his friend wanted to be around him, too.

Because my brother is nice.

My brother is interesting.

He's smart, too.

He knows about keeping the lights off, so we don't waste electricity.

My brother was happy when I said that I thought that was a nice idea. He even gave me a hug without using his hands before he left. But when he came home the next morning, and I hadn't had a bath or washed my hair, he talked really loudly to my mother and sister in the kitchen at breakfast. I think he was talking loudly. He put his headphones on my ears and gave me my breakfast. But he looked like he was talking loudly. He looked like Principal Hoffman after Principal Hoffman walked from one end of the school to the other.

Afterward, he went to his room and stayed there. When I went to his room after breakfast to give him his headphones and asked why he told mom that I hadn't had a bath or washed my hair, why he was trying to get me into trouble, he cried and gave me a hug that lasted a really long time. He accidentally touched me with his hands for four seconds. I didn't like it. But he was sad, so I just touched my fingers to my thumb, and I was okay. And after the really long hug, he played games on his old PS2 with me with the sound turned off for a really long time until I told him I was really bored and ready to get a bath and go to bed. I asked him not to hug me again before bed, and he didn't.

He didn't go hang out with his friend all night anymore. And I guess that made his friend think that my brother didn't want to be his friend anymore, so they stopped being friends. He didn't say he was sad, but I let my brother hug me when he lost his friend. Without using my hands. After I zipped up my hoodie. My brother was really happy that I let him hug me. And he said that he'd be around every night to make sure I got a bath and washed my hair.

I like my brother being around.

I like it when he's at home all night.

I'll be his brother forever.

A Tremendous Amount of Normal

Chapter 2
Will

A Tremendous Amount of Normal

I didn't walk Noah into his first class. But I went with him right up to the door. His first class of the day is World History and his teacher, Mrs. Hess, is an amazing woman. Old as the hills, but she's sharper and more up to date on information about teaching kids like Noah than teachers who are decades younger. Even the teachers freshly certified have nothing on Mrs. Hess. When I walk Noah to his class after the bell has already rung and she sees me with him, she gives me a smile and a wink and goes on teaching as if everything is normal.

Normal is essential to Noah's routine.

Being late was already one blip in his day, we didn't need two so close together.

Mrs. Hess was my saving grace throughout Noah's first three years of high school, and knowing that she would be his history teacher for his senior year was a giant relief. Only once, on Noah's third day as a freshman, did she ask me why she was speaking to me during a teacher's conference instead of Noah's mother and father. Primarly since she had taught me herself in previous years.

There's a significant lack of patience, support, and understanding on my mother's part, and my dad is no longer with us.

That was my response.

Are you Noah's primary caretaker?

Yes.

Are you the person who spends the most time with him outside of his school hours?

Yes.

Every "yes" stung. The look on her face hurt, too. I didn't know how to interpret the way she was looking at me.

Well, she had said, *I'm glad you're here then. Noah is incredibly bright. My God is he sharp. I think he has the textbook memorized already. But I was hoping that you could help me better understand how to communicate with Noah in a way that is easiest and most understandable for him. He really seems to love history and facts, and I think this class could be even more engaging for him if I knew how to present my lesson plans in a way that worked better for him.*

I've never heard a real choir of angels. But that was really close.

Is he asking why a war started?

She nodded.

If he keeps asking and you can't make him understand after the second try, tell him the reason again and then say, 'also, neurotypical people aren't logical.' He understands that.

She laughed.

Will, I think you could explain things more clearly than I could.

We quickly became partners in making sure that Noah got educated as fairly and normally as other students. In Noah's sophomore year, I found out from another teacher that Mrs. Hess had planned to retire after the previous year but had decided to push her retirement out for three more years. When everyone had asked her why she wasn't retiring, she had merely responded:

I just can't imagine retiring at this time.

And she never said anything else about it.

After I saw that Noah had gotten to his seat and cinched his hood around his face, something he could only do in Mrs. Hess' class, I headed to the main office. The halls of the high school, the same one I had graduated from a little over three years prior, looked pretty much the same. Empty hallways between classes still echoed my footsteps, institutional cleaner and hot dog water were the predominate smells, and the lockers were still a royal blue. Noah loved the color of his locker. He loved history—but he really loved his locker.

He had a minor meltdown when he found out that he would have to change lockers each year, so Mrs. Hess and I talked to the principal and made it so Noah could keep the same locker for four years. I say we "talked," but in all actuality, it was a heated debate that went on for far too long. It was bad enough that Noah couldn't bring himself to eat breakfast at school after his middle school years because Principal Sykes wasn't willing to accommodate his extensive dietary needs. But as the years went by, I became more and more aware of the fact that Principal Sykes didn't feel that there was a place in *her school* for kids with special needs.

And her relationship with Mrs. Hess, which had previously been cordial, quickly soured.

She didn't like that Mrs. Hess took my side and not hers.

That just made things harder for Noah.

At least behind the scenes.

One thing I had made clear to Principal Sykes was that she was to take up any problems with me and not question Noah directly. That was another reason why she hated me from the first moment we met.

I missed Principal Hoffman. After his heart attack, he had to retire from his position as principal at the middle school. It hurt my heart when Noah no longer had such a fantastic educator looking after him every school day. He realized that Noah was just Noah and he would always be Noah. He needed the world to modify slightly to fit his particular needs and not act like that was such a big deal. Principal Hoffman was the greatest principal our school district had ever had. He opened a used bookstore to keep himself busy, but less stressed, in his retirement.

My brother is On The Spectrum. That's how they refer to it now. However, Noah was diagnosed with specificity early in life with moderate to severe Asperger Syndrome. I would say that it is severe. Most doctors often shy away from classifying people On The Spectrum as "severe" because that denotes low functionality. Noah's mostly highly functioning but he has a lot of aversions and traits of a person struggling with severe Asperger Syndrome or ASD. In 2013, the DSM V, or *The Diagnostic and Statistical Manual of Mental Disorders 5th Edition*, folded Asperger Syndrome into the all-encompassing category of Autism Spectrum Disorder. So, now everyone says that he is On The Spectrum. Noah doesn't like being referred to as "On The Spectrum"—even if it is true—because he likes the specific of "Asperger Syndrome." Noah likes specificity in general.

On The Spectrum?

Aren't we all somewhere on the line of some spectrum or scale somewhere?

"On The Spectrum" doesn't explain a single thing about my brother.

It's why people call him "retard" or "retarded."

It's why people still use terms like "retard" or "retarded."

Even our own sister—though, I'm trying to think of a better term for my relationship with her—calls Noah "retard" when he frustrates her. What does he do to frustrate her?

He walks.

He talks.

He breathes.

He exists.

She's a fucking bitch and has as little concern for Noah as our mother does. I wish she were actually another brother so that I could punch her in her prissy face until I felt bones shatter. Not that violence solves much, but the way people refuse to change even slightly to make life less difficult for Noah is infuriating at times.

Luckily, Noah doesn't understand.

At least, not entirely.

He knows what the term "retard" means.

Just like he knows the literal meaning of most words.

But he doesn't know how someone thinks that he is mentally handicapped or that the term "retard" can be a cruel insult.

It's the same way when someone says a racial slur.

Or when my sister calls me "fag."

He doesn't understand sarcasm.

Or satire.

Or insincerity.

Or hyperbole.

Or cruelty.

My brother is normal. He is filled with an overabundance of normal. That's the problem. He's incredibly normal. He says what he means, and he means what he says. He is precise. When he describes someone, it's factual. Not intended to be hurtful. He may say that he is looking for "that fat guy with a big nose and no hair." He doesn't see these as insults or insulting. The guy just happened to be overweight, have a large nose, and been bald. That is no different to him than saying the sky is blue and the grass is green or the Gatorade flavor he likes best is the "blue kind that he supposes tastes like a frozen glacier" though he "wouldn't know since he's never tasted a glacier."

He's never called someone "ugly."

You'll hear:

Fat.

Black.

White.

Mexican.

Asian.

Tall.

Short.

Skinny.

Big feet.

Big nose.

Freckles.

Loud voice.

He says "really" a lot.

Like "really loud" or "really bright" or "really big."

"Really scary."

Most things are "really" to him. Nothing is an acceptable level of noisy or quiet or light or dark or soft or hard or cold or hot. Everything falls to the left or right of the middle of a scale. The only thing that is perfect to him is "purple grape jelly without pieces of grape in it." He's perpetually like Goldilocks stumbling upon the bears' home—before Baby Bear was born. With my brother, we live in a universe where Baby Bear will never be born. Everything will be too much of one thing or another, and he has to learn how to make that work for him.

He adjusts himself, like any other person. He lets hot soup sit on the table for twenty minutes and stares at it until it is the perfect temperature. He keeps spreading the jelly on his plain bread until it is in a thin, even layer over the entirety of the bread. He will pick any leftover pith off of a peeled orange until there is none left. He will use his spoon to ladle minuscule portions of milk out of his cereal bowl until the perfect ratio of milk to cereal remains. But then the soup is too cold by the time he gets halfway done. The jelly is getting too gelatinous on the edge of the bread he started on. The skin of the orange will get picked away with some of the pith, exposing some of the juicy flesh. The cereal is now soggy after the ten minutes he took to ladle out milk.

So, I've had to make adjustments. I've learned to put one cup of cereal with one-half cup of milk. I buy Cuties, so that peeling regular oranges is no longer a problem. I have learned to call Noah to the table when the soup is lukewarm—and then how to reheat it back to lukewarm in the microwave when he is half done. I've found a brand of jelly that doesn't get weirdly thicker quickly when exposed to air.

Everything about my brother is normal. But nothing in this world works at the same speed of normal as him. He's either too late or too early. And then things become not normal.

I rubbed my split knuckles as I walked down the hallway towards the office. In a rush to stop my brother from banging his head against the table, I didn't wrap the kitchen towel completely around my hand. When I put my hand against his forehead, and his head went down again, he slammed my hand into the table as well. He was going so quickly that he managed to bang my hand into the table three times before I could wrap him up in my arms.

After I talked to the principal, and before I went to my first class, I would have to stop at the pharmacy for bandages. Just like the oranges, we were out. That is why I hadn't been able to cover up the knot on Noah's head that would surely be purple when I picked him up after school. Speaking to Principal Sykes immediately would help to stave off any extra attention his bruise would get. Mrs. Hess would probably send a note with Noah to his second class, but I couldn't rely on the teacher in his second class to keep the chain going.

"I need to see Principal Sykes," I announced to her secretary as I entered her office.

There was no reason to make pleasantries. They'd make none with me. This wasn't the first time I'd been in this office.

"What do you need to talk to me about now?" Principal Sykes appeared at the open doorway of her office, looking at me over her seated secretary.

"Well, it's never anything but my brother, is it?" I replied evenly.

A hand motion was her only indication that she was listening.

"He has a knot on his forehead this morning," I stated blandly. "It'll probably be pretty noticeable by the end of the day. And his lip is split."

Her eyes landed on my knuckles.

I rolled my eyes.

"He had anxiety this morning," I spoke through clenched teeth. "I had to stop him from banging his head on the table."

"Did you have to be violent about it?"

"I've never hit my brother," I stated evenly. "And I imagine that you are just smart enough to know not to imply otherwise, Principal Sykes."

She glared at me.

"My brother knows how to tell the truth," I added. "Regardless of what you think of his abilities."

"Is there anything else?" She snapped.

"Yeah. This place still smells like a privately funded maximum-security prison." I replied.

Then I left.

Leaving the high school after I've dropped off Noah is really easy—as Noah might say. Leaving in general, maybe not so much. It doesn't run in the family. My sister left her compassion in the womb. My mother left her good emotions in the trunk of the car. The car my dad left in the day I graduated high school. Noah never leaves because he was never there. He never promised me anything. Well, that's not true.

When he was much younger, really young, he was incredibly highly functioning for a kid like him in his age group.

I'll be your brother forever, Will. I'll be your best friend forever.

That he promised me.

I'll be your brother and best friend forever, too, Noah.

I promised that out loud. Internally, many years later, as I played games with him so that he wouldn't see my dad driving away, I mentally promised to never leave. If it had just been my mother and sister—I would've taken a cue from my dad. Noah, though. Noah is not my sister or my mother. He loves me in one of the purest ways. In

34

the only way he knows how. He tells the truth. He says what he means. He means what he says. He communicates in a way that you don't have to detect sarcasm or irony or lies. Noah is my normal. I've never wanted any other kind of normal.

A Tremendous Amount of Normal

Chapter 3

Noah

A Tremendous Amount of Normal

Sometimes my brother brings me a rock when he picks me up from school. At his college, they have a manmade pond filled with Koi fish. It's right by the really big sign at the front of the school where you pull into the parking lot. At the bottom of the pond, there are lots of really colorful rocks that the Koi move with their mouths when they are searching for food. Over the years, the rocks have been worn smooth by the fish sucking on them as they move them. Some are red.

Blue.

Green.

White.

Beige.

I suppose it's like the gravel in aquariums, but they're bigger. I like the way they feel in the palm of my hand. It's like holding someone else's hand but not having to be touched by rough skin that is covered in hair. They're really pretty, too. Usually, they're really shiny. My brother tells me he picks out the shiniest and prettiest rock he can find in the entire pond. I think that is probably a very nice thing to do.

Mrs. Hess is really old. She stands with me while I wait for my brother outside of my school. But she's smart like Principal Hoffman was. She told me that cinching my hood around my head when we went outside into the really bright sun would help protect me from getting a sunburn. She's right. But she also says that UV rays are what causes sunburns. It's only UVA and UVB rays that cause sunburn because UVC rays do not reach the Earth's surface. I told my brother this, and he told me that Mrs. Hess just forgot to mention the part about UVC rays, so she was mostly right.

I suppose he's right.

My brother understands people better than I do.

So, I told Mrs. Hess about UVC rays the next day and that my brother said she probably just forgot to mention they didn't reach the Earth's surface so she was actually right.

Mrs. Hess said my brother is a very good brother.

I laughed at that because it was funny.

Obviously, my brother is a very good brother.

Mrs. Hess is okay at hugging, too.

When my brother's car pulls up in front of us each day, Mrs. Hess pats me on the back with her forearm, and her hand never touches me. Her hugs are rhythmic and firm, and she never turns her mouth to my ear to tell me "goodbye." I like her hugs, too. But she's not as good at hugging as my brother. She always tells me that she will see me as soon as I get to school the next day and that we'll wait for my brother after school again.

That doesn't make sense to me.

Of course, I'll see her when I get to school.

She teaches my World History class, which is my first class of the day.

And I am not waiting for my brother after school.

I start waiting for him as soon as he drops me off in the morning.

One time, in Mrs. Hess' class during junior year, every student was allowed to invite their parents to come talk about what they did to earn money. My mom was really busy, and my dad hasn't been home in one-thousand-two-hundred-and-thirty-seven days. Mrs. Hess asked me if my brother would want to come talk about what he is studying in college.

My brother studies electrical engineering in college. He says that it is a good degree plan and it will help him make enough money in the future. I'm not sure what he needs a lot of money for since he lives with us at our home, but he doesn't like to talk about it. But I suppose that if it makes him happy, then it is probably a nice thing. He takes a lot of math and science classes at college.

I like that.

I like talking about numbers.

He's really good with computers and cell phones.

So, that's interesting.

My brother didn't talk about what he studied in college. He went to the front of the class to start talking about what he studied, but that was all. He told everyone who he was, and then some kid in the back of the class said something about mental retardation that I didn't really understand. My brother started looking like Principal Hoffman when Principal Hoffman walked from one end of the school to the other. Then he said the kid was a "worthless piece of shit bastard" and Mrs. Hess made him leave the room to "cool off."

To "cool off" means to calm down.

That's what Mrs. Hess told me after school that day.

Then Mrs. Hess made the kid go to the Principal's office to talk to the principal.

But he came back in seven minutes.

I suppose the Principal didn't have much to tell him.

It takes two minutes and thirty-seven seconds to walk to the Principal's office at my school.

He was smiling at Mrs. Hess, even though she was frowning at him.

So, I think everything was okay.

I still don't really understand why my brother said what he said to that kid.

I understand what "worthless" is, but I don't think that any kid in my class is worthless.

A lot of them don't use their full potential.

I've seen their grades.

I did an internet search for "piece of shit" because I was sure the dictionary was wrong, and I found out that it means "someone who is a horrible person."

That is an insult.

I don't think my brother meant to insult anyone.

My brother is probably really nice to everyone.

But I don't know why my brother called the kid a "bastard."

His father had just talked to the class the day before my brother did.

When Mrs. Hess hugs me when I get into my brother's car, I am really happy. My brother always has the air conditioner on in his car when it is warm outside. He says that he likes it cold so that he is comfortable. Which I like, too. He has a CD that plays my favorite song over and over when we drive home. I like that, too. It's a song called *Porcelain* by a singer called Moby. Which is really funny when you think about it. And my brother plays it on number four volume. I think that is the perfect volume to listen to the song.

I like that my brother likes the same song as me and likes it played at number four on the volume.

My brother does the same thing every time he picks me up.

He asks me if I was good in school.

Which is really funny when you think about it.

I'm good at school.

How are you good in school?

Every day I tell him this.

That always makes him smile, and he asks me if I was nice to other people and behaved in my classes. When I tell him that I was, he gives me a gift. Almost always a rock from the manmade pond at the front of his school by the big sign. Sometimes he brings me the snack crackers that taste like butter and have smooth peanut butter between them. I don't like the other kind with the chalky peanut butter in them. Then he promises that we'll go together to see the manmade pond that the Koi live in someday.

I ask my brother how many days until we go see the fish.

He tells me that we'll go in 297 days.

Which is funny.

He's said that every day for one-thousand-one-hundred-and-forty-four days.

My brother probably does so much math in college that he has trouble doing it when we're in the car.

Sometimes, when my brother picks me up from school, we can't go home. I don't really know why because we go home and mom's car is there. The car is parked really weird where the front tires are in the yard. But my brother says that mom is busy cleaning the house when that happens, so we go somewhere else for two to three hours. It's kind of funny because the living room is not clean when we get home. But you can tell that mom was trying because she moves a lot of things around and she always falls asleep on the couch from cleaning so hard.

My brother gets sad.

Which I can understand.

Mom is so tired from cleaning that he has to take her to her bedroom.

And after he helps me get my bath and wash my hair, he has to finish cleaning for her.

She never says anything to my brother about finishing the cleaning the next morning, but I know that she is glad that he did it.

It's probably very nice of him.

I like it when mom is cleaning when we get home, even if it makes my brother sad.

My brother takes us to a restaurant on the other side of town that makes really good pancakes. It's a really quiet place, and there's never more than nine other people there when we go. Both sides of the pancakes are always the same color of brown, and the syrup jars are never sticky. I like that. The sausages that they give me are the patties that come frozen in a box, not the links. Which I like. And the eggs are always made sunny-side up without crispy brown edges. I like that, too. They also have skim milk so that I don't have to drink water. I told the waitress that she looked really old, but my brother told me and her that she wasn't old and that she looked like she was barely old enough to drive. My brother told the waitress that it's hard for me to tell how old people are because I'm special. Which was interesting. The second time we went to the restaurant, the waitress gave me a Rubik's Cube to play with. She brings it to work with her every time in case mom is cleaning that day. It's kind of funny because if she's not there, the other waitresses always have a Rubik's Cube, too. I suppose they all really like playing with them, too.

I don't like water from other people's houses.

Or at restaurants.

It tastes weird.

My brother always gets coffee. I don't like coffee. It tastes dirty and burnt on my tongue, and it's always really hot. One time my brother got a cup and filled it halfway up with coffee and then filled it the rest of the way up with skim milk and put sugar in it and gave it to me. I really liked that. But he only let me have a few sips of the coffee because he said it wasn't good for me.

People on the spectrum aren't supposed to have caffeine.

Coffee has caffeine in it.

If I drink coffee, it can make me anxious.

And not sleep.

But it was probably really nice that my brother let me taste the coffee with milk and sugar.

It didn't keep me awake or make me anxious.

My brother tells me that if anyone calls me "retarded" that I should tell them that I'm on the spectrum.

"On the spectrum" means that a person has Autism Spectrum Disorder.

That's not correct.

I have Asperger Syndrome, which affects approximately 1 in 200 people. Autism Spectrum Disorders affect approximately 1 in 110 people. I have Asperger Syndrome, not Autism Spectrum Disorder. Asperger Syndrome is a milder type of Autism, but I was diagnosed as having Asperger Syndrome. I don't like it when people don't use my diagnosis. My brother says that neurotypical people don't understand that, so if I tell them that I am on the spectrum, then they will understand it better.

Explaining things to neurotypical people is really difficult.

I am not good at that like I am with numbers and history.

But my brother lets me say Asperger Syndrome when I'm talking to him because he understands. I don't think he's like other neurotypical people. He's a lot smarter than other neurotypicals, I suppose. He explains to me that neurotypical people and even some people who have Asperger Syndrome and Autism Spectrum Disorder will tell me I am wrong for feeling the way that I feel, but I shouldn't let that bother me because everyone has a right to feel the way they feel about "their own tribes."

I'm not entirely sure what that means, but I think I mostly understand.

I think he means that I don't always have to have the same feelings as other people and that is okay.

When my brother takes me to the pancake restaurant, he gets something different to eat every time. It's kind of funny when you think about it. One time he said the meatloaf wasn't as good as the fried chicken. And the fried chicken wasn't as good as the chicken and dumplings. I asked him why he didn't get chicken and dumplings every time since they were the best. He told me that he won't know what is good unless he tries everything.

I don't really understand that.

The pancakes are always good.

And the syrup jars are never sticky.

Why would someone want to try something different that might not be as good as the last thing that you had?

My brother is interesting.

A Tremendous Amount of Normal

Chapter 4
Will

A Tremendous Amount of Normal

"Do you need me to stay in here with you, Noah?" I asked as I turned off the tub faucet.

Noah doesn't like to have the bath water run before he gets into the tub. Immersing himself into water in one go is too much sensation. He has to get into the tub when it is empty and let it fill up around him. It's easier for him to adjust to the temperature of the water and the feeling against his skin bit by bit.

"Why would I need you to stay in here?"

"Do you want me to stay in here with you, Noah?" I changed the question as I stood beside the tub.

This question takes longer to answer. Noah has to think about what he is feeling if the question is a "feeling" question.

"No."

"Okay," I replied. "I'll be back in ten minutes. Make sure to clean your armpits, your penis and testicles, and your butt."

"In that order. After everything else."

"In that order. After everything else." I parroted.

My brother is not dumb. He's incredibly intelligent. But certain things, like putting a wash rag near your butt and then putting it near another body part defeats the purpose of getting clean, are difficult for him to grasp at times. Which makes me laugh to myself because he refuses to touch stairway railings unless they're in our home. But that's the thing. His germs are his germs. No matter where they are on his body. To him, germs and bacteria from his butt are no different than the ones in his nose or ears. Even though he knows there are bacteria in his butt that could make him sick, he forgets that his bacteria and germs can still be harmful to him. They're *his* bacteria and germs.

He's incredibly good about remembering the harm in his own bacteria and germs now, but I remind him at bath time, just to be sure. I'm probably overly cautious, but Noah is my world.

I left Noah to clean himself in the bathtub and shut the door until it was open only about six inches. Just in case he needed to scream for me. That happens sometimes. I set the timer on my phone for ten minutes, just as I had told Noah, and then went downstairs to clean up my mom's mess. Luckily, she was already fairly loaded when she got to the house this time, so she only threw a few things before falling out on the couch. Mostly, I just had to put books back on the shelves, put a few knick-knacks back where they belonged and straighten the lampshade. I fluffed the cushions and pillows on the couch and considered the job done.

Then I went into the kitchen to make sure that we had everything that Noah would need for breakfast. Noah and I had picked up oranges at the store on the way home, thankfully, so that solved the pear problem. However, when I checked the cabinet, all of the bread was gone. More than likely, our sister had decided that her hunger was more important than Noah's routine.

Our sister is a year older than Noah. She is supposed to be going to one of the local community colleges, but mostly I think she hangs out with her boyfriend. She's rarely ever home when we are, so that is a blessing. Though, there's no doubt that my mother would rather have our sister home than Noah and me. That was also a blessing because it made it easier to hate her. It also made me happy that we were making her unhappy with our presence.

Once Noah was asleep, I'd have to go to the corner store for a loaf of bread. I made a quick decision and grabbed the grape jelly, the almonds, and the oranges and carried them up to my room. When I bought bread, it was going in my room, too. I wasn't going to let our mother and sister keep doing this to Noah. The only thing I couldn't keep in my room was the skim milk—but they didn't like that anyway, so there wasn't a huge chance that they'd drink it and ruin Noah's routine.

I peeked my head in to make sure my mom was still fully clothed and passed out on top of her bed where I had left her. When I had closed her door again, the timer on my phone went off. Noah was sitting in the tub expectantly when I went in to check on him.

"Did you clean everything?" I asked, reaching for his microfiber towel that hung on the back of the bathroom door.

"Yes."

"Are you ready to wash your hair?" I asked, reaching down to pull the plug out of the tub drain.

I stood and held the towel open for Noah. Noah stood from the tub carefully. He doesn't like it when water splashes over the side and puddles on the floor. He doesn't like to stand in puddles. He stepped out of the tub and into the towel, and I draped it around him, making sure to not touch him with my hands. Noah took the towel from me and wrapped it around himself like a big blanket.

"Am I gross, Will?" Noah asked once he had turned around, shivering slightly under the towel.

Noah is sensitive to temperature, but cold doesn't make him anxious like hot does.   His bathwater has to be just warm enough to get him clean but not so warm that it makes him feel like his skin is boiling.

"You are not gross, Noah," I replied.

I wanted to laugh.

But you don't laugh at Noah's questions.

They're not jokes.

"Thomas Johnson said that I was gross," Noah said. "Gross means very obvious and unacceptable. Or extremely unpleasant. It can also mean without deduction of tax or other contributions. I think he meant that I'm unacceptable or extremely unpleasant."

"Thomas Johnson is a little…" I began.

I have to stop myself a lot when I try to explain people to Noah.

"Thomas Johnson was wrong." I tried to smile as I used my forearms to press the towel against Noah's skin.

"I think so, too," Noah replied. "He also said I was a retard again. I told him again that I'm not retarded, but he keeps saying it. I suppose he just doesn't understand words like you do."

"I'm definitely smarter than Thomas Johnson," I replied.

"Obviously. Did you know that he lost his virginity when he was twelve and that I'll never lose my virginity?"

"Thomas Johnson didn't lose his virginity at twelve and he never will." I corrected him. "And why do you think that you'll never lose your virginity, Noah?"

"To lose one's virginity, one has to participate in sexual intercourse," Noah replied. "One's body is pressed against another person's body, and the penis is inserted into the vagina, mouth, or anus, and copulation is completed."

"There's a little more to it than that," I stated. "But if you find a girl who you want to have sex with one day, we'll explain to her that you don't like to be touched in certain ways."

"Do you need to touch people with your hands to have sexual intercourse?"

"Not necessarily," I explained. "Do you want to lose your virginity one day?"

This was a feeling question. Noah had to think while I dried him off without using my hands. Noah can dry himself off—he's not incapable. But it takes him a really long time, and it would be just as sensible for him to air dry—but then there are puddles on the floor, and he doesn't like puddles. Noah can't run his hands over his chest, back, thighs, and feet too rapidly or for too long without getting anxious. Even if a towel is between his hands and his body. Fingertips make him anxious if they touch most parts of his body. Conversations with Noah would be awkward with anyone else. In fact, once Noah first became aware of sex, and what that entailed, it was uncomfortable with him, too. But just like someone being fat is factual to Noah, sex is just a topic to discuss and examine. It's not titillating or perverse. It's just another function that the human body performs that he wants to understand.

"If a girl were hygienic, I would want to lose my virginity." He stated. "And if she didn't touch me with her hands. Or kiss me."

It was a struggle not to laugh. I settled for a wide smile.

"Well, we'll find you a really clean girl who won't touch you with her hands or kiss you, Noah."

"Do I need a haircut?"

Topics change often and quickly with Noah.

"Thomas Johnson said that my hair was too long and I look like a fag."

"You don't look like a fag, Noah," I responded through clenched teeth again.

"People call me a fag a lot," Noah stated. "Do they mean it is a bad thing?"

I sighed.

"A fag is a guy who is a homosexual, Noah."

"So, it's not a bad thing." Noah wasn't asking a question.

"Right." I smiled. "But people call homosexuals 'fags' if they don't like homosexuals and they think it is bad. But you can't say someone is a homosexual because of their hair because homosexuals have all different colors and styles of hair. Or none at all."

"Then how do you know that I don't look like a fag?"

"Because you just look like a Noah," I replied. "You look the way that you are supposed to look—nothing else."

"Are you a homosexual?" Noah asked.

"Why do you ask?" I reached for Noah's pajamas.

"Because Jennifer calls you a fag when she's angry."

"Yes, Noah," I replied. "I am a homosexual. But most people use the term "gay" now."

"Do you like my hair?" Noah asked. "As a homosexual?"

"Can't I just appreciate it as another human being?"

"Yes," Noah replied. "You can appreciate it. But as a homosexual who finds other males attractive, do you like my hair?"

"Your hair is very nice, Noah," I replied. "You're my handsomest brother."

"I'm your only brother." Noah looked thoughtful for a moment. "Would other homosexuals like my hair?"

I couldn't help but laugh.

"I'm sure some would."

"Then logically, heterosexual girls would, too," Noah stated. "Right?"

"Yes. Well, some of them." I held Noah's pajamas out to him.

"I want to know which girls like my hair."

"Do you want a girlfriend?"

"No." Noah handed me his towel to hang up as he took his pajamas from me. "They would want me to kiss them and hug them and touch me with their hands. But I would enjoy seeing breasts."

"Well," I turned to hang the towel up, "you can't ask a girl to show you her breasts unless you know that she really likes you and wants to do sex things with you."

"Why not?" Noah asked as he pulled on his pajama bottoms. "I like breasts, and I can't see them unless a girl shows me. Girls have breasts. And if she liked my hair, it would be symbiotic."

"Neurotypical people often don't understand symbiosis as a sexual concept, Noah," I explained as he pulled his t-shirt over his head.

I immediately reached up to smooth his bangs away from his forehead with my forearm.

"Sex is an emotional act. It involves love or at least feelings that one person likes another." I continued. "Sex isn't a transaction."

"By definition it is."

I frowned to myself as I closed the toilet lid and sat down. Noah watched my actions and then lowered himself to sit rigidly on the side of the tub. I prayed that the side of the tub was not damp. The whole bathing process might have to be repeated.

"A transaction between two people is unemotional," I explained. "Like when I paid for our food or bought the oranges. I give money, and I get food and oranges. That's all. When you have sex with someone, you are exchanging emotions. Sometimes it's love, but it can also be happiness or joy or sorrow or guilt or lust or compassion or comfort. But no matter what it is—it's not unemotional at all. Neurotypical people don't often understand that sex can simply be done to feel good physically. You have to at least like the other person to have sex."

"I would like a girl if I had sex with her."

"You want to like her before you have sex with her." I smiled. "Then sex with her will be good."

"Won't it feel good anyway?"

I thought about this.

"You don't want to kiss a girl or hug a girl or let her touch you with her hands?"

"No."

"How will she know these things if you aren't at least friends, Noah?"

He thought about this.

"So, a girl I like and am friends with will know how to have sex the way I like it?"

"Precisely. And you will know how she likes to have sex."

"And, since we like each other and like how we have sex, she'll want to have sex again."

"Well, maybe."

"When you have sex with a guy, do you want to have sex with him again?"

"Not that I have a ton of experience." I tried not to roll my eyes. Noah doesn't understand eye rolling. "But no. I don't always want to have sex with a guy again after we've had sex once."

"Why not?"

"Sometimes it turns out that I don't like him as much as I thought I did."

Noah didn't respond. This usually means that Noah has understood everything and he has no further questions.

"Ready to wash your hair?"

"Yes."

"Let's go." I motioned towards the door.

"Don't use the green shampoo, Will," Noah stated. "I like the one that is honey-colored. The green one smells like pine trees."

"I'll use the honey-colored shampoo, Noah."

"I don't want you to hug me before bed."

"No hugs," I replied. "I promise."

Once, when Noah was ten years old, my sister put dog shampoo in his hair. And it got in his eyes. He hasn't forgotten it.   He likes the "honey-colored shampoo" that "smells like oranges and honeysuckle."

So, I washed Noah's hair in the kitchen sink with the right shampoo—which is always tricky since I can only use my wrists and forearms. I dried it thoroughly with the hairdryer set on the cool setting—which makes drying his hair take forever as he keeps his head held in the sink so that it doesn't drip on him—and then got him to bed. His curtains had shifted slightly, leaving a small gap where he could see the streetlight outside, so I had to fix that for him. But, all in all, putting him to bed took less time than it usually did.

Once I was sure that he was asleep, I checked to make sure that my mom was still passed out in her room and grabbed my keys, phone, and wallet, and headed to the store. Our house isn't too far from the university, which means there is a lot of college housing nearby. Luckily, this translates to a lot of businesses nearby, including a store a half mile away that is pretty well stocked. If Noah weren't at home asleep, I would have taken the opportunity to walk. But since I didn't want to leave him alone with our drunk and passed out mother for too long, I drove to the store.

The corner store—where I do a lot of last-minute shopping—is open twenty-four hours a day and is a bastion of LED lights and noise. College kids nearby, remember? But they have the bread that Noah likes. The wheat kind without seeds or flecks of brown things in it. It has a thin crust. It doesn't crumble too much when he bites into it, and it doesn't get soggy from the purple grape jelly without grape pieces in it like white bread does.

Noah likes coming to the store with me if there are not too many people because he likes to look at all of the bags of bread that are available. There's a whole wall full of regular breads to ethnic breads to specialty breads. He can look at them for several minutes—but he always picks the same bread. Regardless, he likes seeing the variety of breads that are available in this store. But if there are too many people in the store, there is too much noise. Combined with the lights, he can't tolerate the store during peak hours.

As I stood in front of the wall of bread, I realized that it would have been an excellent time to bring Noah to the store. The only people I saw were a few straggling customers and the staff, which was minimal at ten o'clock on a Thursday. The next thing I realized was that the place where Noah's favorite bread was usually stocked was utterly empty. A depressing cubbyhole of emptiness that made me consider having my own little meltdown for once. I looked at the empty shelf, and my stomach sank. The bread might be in stock at another large chain grocery store in town. But…if I spent a lot of time searching for the bread, that would be time Noah was alone in the house with our mother. And if I spent all that time searching for a bag of the bread and didn't find any—there would be another meltdown before school.

Then I might have busted knuckles again.

Then I'd have to talk to Principal Sykes.

Then the meltdowns would get more frequent.

If Noah starts having regular meltdowns, they increase with frequency and severity.

I didn't want Noah to have another slightly noticeable scar from banging his head.

Noah is a handsome boy. If he were a neurotypical boy, the girls would be swarming him like flies on shit. But he was On The Spectrum. And he had a small scar on his forehead and on his cheek. And teenage girls can be cruel. I didn't want Noah to be anything but who he was, but I didn't like that life was so hard for him. Correction: I didn't like that people were so cruel to him. I took deep breaths as I stood and looked at the empty space on the shelf.

"What are you doing here?"

I jumped at the sound of the voice and whipped my head to the side. The voice came from another student in my Integrated Electronics course. He had a shopping basket draped over his forearm, smiling at my reaction as he stood there.

"You scared the shit out of me, Manny." I laughed.

"I see that." He smiled mischievously. "Can you not decide on one out of two thousand types of bread?"

I laughed. "Have you started working on your project for Professor Avery yet?"

He shook his head. "Well, yes. But I'm still looking for a partner."

"You may be in luck." I smiled goofily. "I haven't started yet, and I need a partner, too, so it would be great if I could jump in and benefit from your work ethic."

Manny laughed.

"Deal." He held out his hand. "Symbiosis, man."

I shook his hand. "I'm bringing nothing to the table."

"Your partnership." He explained. "Besides, I know that you're doing well in Avery's class, so eventually you would have started and knocked it out of the park. And…"

His eyes darted back and forth.

"What?"

"Avery doesn't care for brown people much." He sighed but gave a smile that conveyed years of getting accustomed to this type of prejudice. "So, you can bring the overall skin tone of our duo down several shades."

"How dare you be Indian?" I smiled sadly with him.

He shrugged. "I'm from Vermont. Fuck me for having Indian parents, right?"

I laughed loudly.

"Bastard. How dare you?"

"I know." He shook his head ruefully. "So, how about starting tomorrow? I have time after class."

"I have to work in the university store before I pick my brother up from school." I chewed at my lip. "But how about tomorrow evening? I know this quiet pancake place, so we could easily meet there. The food and coffee are awful, but, ya' know."

"That sounds awesome." He replied, then turned towards the bread. "So, which one are you getting? How white are you?"

I snorted. "I'm not getting Wonder bread if that's what you're thinking."

"I never would have thought such a thing."

"I'd get that one there." I pointed.

"Pumpernickel?" Manny nodded slowly. "I'm impressed. It's not the bread of my people, but I respect that you chose something dark."

I laughed again. "I like that's it's kind of sweet and tangy. And dense. It's complex."

"So, grab a bag." He motioned with his head.

"I'm not here for me." I shook my head. "I was here to get bread for my brother's breakfast, but they're all out."

My eyes landed on the empty shelf space again and my stomach sunk another few inches. I was wasting bread searching time.

"He will only eat one kind."

Manny didn't reply verbally. He reached into his basket and pulled out a loaf of the bread that I had been looking for when I entered the store.

"You bread thief." I laughed nervously.

"For your brother." He held it out to me.

"No." I chewed at my bottom lip. "I couldn't."

"Take it." He held his arm closer. "I think I'll get pumpernickel."

I took the bag from him.

"Thank you." I looked down, so very grateful. "I didn't really want to try every other store in town."

"You're welcome. I have younger brothers, too."

"How old are your brothers?" I asked as I cradled the loaf of bread in my arm.

You need to get home to Noah, dude.

"Rajesh is sixteen, Vijay is twelve, and Deepak is turning ten next month. I have an older brother, too. Sai. He's twenty-five and has his MBA from Harvard. My parents are incredibly proud, obviously." He beamed as he spoke. "Deepak wants to become an electrical engineer, too, because obviously, I'm the coolest guy he knows. For now.

He'll probably end up wanting to be an actor or something in a few years."

"I don't know." I shrugged. "You'll probably stay cool long enough to see him get an electrical engineering degree."

"We can hope." He laughed. "How old is your brother?"

I looked down at my watch so that I could get out of this.

"Oh, shit." I grimaced. "I have to get home. We'll talk tomorrow if that's okay?"

"Of course."

"I really *really* appreciate this." I motioned with the bread in my arm. "It's already making my life easier."

"Anytime." He nodded. "See you in Avery's tomorrow."

"See ya'." I agreed.

I paid and went home. A loaf of bread got hidden on the top shelf of my closet, next to almonds without the skins, and purple grape jelly without the grape pieces. And then I was in bed sound asleep.

Chapter 5

Noah

A Tremendous Amount of Normal

Our mom was cleaning again in the morning, and Will was trying to help her when I went downstairs for breakfast the next morning. They weren't working well together. Mom kept throwing stuff to the other side of the room, and Will was trying to put things back where they came from. It didn't seem like the smartest way to clean to me, but I don't understand neurotypical people most of the time. It was really loud when the things my mom threw landed. And she was screaming about hating everything in the house.

If I hated everything in the house, I would probably be screaming, too.

Will wasn't screaming at our mom, but he looked like Principal Hoffman when Principal Hoffman walked from one end of the school to the other.

After putting several things back where they had been before our mom had thrown them, he sat my mother down on the couch really roughly.

He said something that I didn't understand.

He said she was a "fucking bitch" and a "worthless mother."

I know what a "fucking bitch" is.

I learned that in seventh grade when Katie Spencer called Alice King a "fucking bitch."

My brother explained to me what it meant when he picked me up from school that day.

It's a really mean thing to call another person.

I don't know why my brother would call our mom that.

I don't think our mom is worthless.

She used to take me to the doctor.

She took me to get stitches when I was bleeding.

That is probably a very nice thing she did.

And it wasn't worthless.

I asked if I could help and for some reason, my brother and our mom got really scared and jumped up. Our mom started crying and almost touched me when she ran back up the stairs. Then she slammed the door to her bedroom. I heard her scream that my brother was a fag.

My brother is not a fag.

He's a homosexual.

Gay. My brother is gay.

A fag is what you call a gay man if you do not like gay men.

Fags are bad, gay men are not.

My brother is the best brother in the world.

I'll be his brother forever.

My brother asked me if I slept well. I did sleep well. I told him so. He looked very sad, even though he was smiling. I zipped up my hoodie and asked if he wanted to hug me. He said that I didn't have to if I didn't want to. I think that was probably very nice because I didn't want to hug anyone then. I told him I didn't want to hug anyone.

He told me that I was the best Noah in the world.

I told him he was the best Will that I knew.

We had breakfast. I had almonds without the skins, an orange that my brother peeled for me, a glass of skim milk, and a slice of bread with purple grape jelly without the grape pieces. It was really good. The bread was the first slice after the heel, which is always the best piece. I told my brother that he could have the next slice, which is the second-best slice, but he told me that he wanted to save it for me.

I think that was probably very nice of him.

My brother likes to drink a very big cup of coffee and eat scrambled eggs and toast. I don't like toast because crumbs get on my shirt and stuck between my teeth and my cheeks. Eggs aren't good scrambled. Then they're yellow all over. The yolk is yellow, and the albumen is white. Scrambled eggs are just yellow. That is really funny when you think about it.

When my brother took me to school, he asked me if I wanted him to walk me to class and I said "yes." I like it when my brother walks me to class, especially if the bell hasn't rung yet. The other kids don't scream questions at me that I don't understand and don't know the answers to when he walks with me. And he doesn't get mad at me for keeping my hood cinched tightly around my head when we're walking through the halls.

When my brother walks me to Mrs. Hess class before the bell rings, Mrs. Hess talks to him and laughs a lot as they wait on the other kids to show up. Right before class starts, Mrs. Hess tells him that he has to hug her before he leaves. When my brother hugs Mrs. Hess, his chest touches her chest, and he puts his arms around her, and his hands touch her back. The sides of their heads touch and they rock back and forth very slightly. That's very interesting. My brother doesn't like hugging people that way. But I have never really seen him hug anyone but Mrs. Hess and me.

My brother gives the best hugs in the world.

But maybe he saves the best hugs for me.

Just like the second-best slice of bread.

When my brother left Mrs. Hess' class, Thomas Johnson almost ran into him in the doorway. My brother looked like Principal Hoffman again, and he got really big and moved through the doorway so that Thomas Johnson couldn't enter. Mrs. Hess left the room quickly then and closed the door as the bell rang. Thirty-seven seconds later, Mrs. Hess opened the door and came back into class, and Thomas Johnson followed her. My brother wasn't with them. Thomas Johnson looked anxious and was watching his feet as he walked to his seat. Mrs. Hess looked anxious, too, but she was smiling in a really unusual way.

My brother probably said something really nice.

I think he probably told Thomas Johnson that it was okay that he didn't understand words.

Because neurotypical people aren't really smart sometimes.

Not like my brother is.

But Thomas Johnson didn't talk to me the rest of the day.

After school was over, Mrs. Hess waited for me at the front of the school. Mrs. Hess told me that I have the best brother in the world. I told Mrs. Hess that she was right. Mrs. Hess told me that I should always be nice to my brother. I told Mrs. Hess that I'm never mean to my brother. I told Mrs. Hess that my brother wasn't a fag that he was a gay man because people who don't like gay men call them fags and gay men are not bad.

Mrs. Hess told me she wanted to tell me a secret but only if I knew how to keep a secret.

I laughed at that.

Obviously, I know how to keep a secret.

Mrs. Hess told me that she doesn't think that my brother is a fag either.

Because my brother is the best brother in the world.

Mrs. Hess told me that she thinks that my brother is the best person she knows and I should love my brother.

I told her my brother was the best Will that I knew.

Then my brother's car showed up, and Mrs. Hess gave me a hug with her forearm against my back.

Mrs. Hess' hugs are not as good as my brother's.

But I don't mind too much when she hugs me.

Mrs. Hess opened the car for me and shut it behind me.

Mrs. Hess told my brother "goodbye" through the window, without leaning in and putting her face near mine. I don't like that.

I told my brother that Mrs. Hess didn't think he was a fag either and he was the best person that she knew.

Mrs. Hess and my brother got really quiet, which I didn't understand.

Then my brother finally told Mrs. Hess "thank you" and his voice sounded funny.

Mrs. Hess nodded and walked away.

Her face looked really red.

My brother didn't drive his car away from the school. Which is really funny when you think about it. I think he forgot how to drive for the twenty-nine seconds that we sat there. It doesn't seem that hard to do, but I'm not allowed to drive. I don't really want to drive. One time I tried to drive and other cars were always honking really loudly then, and I didn't like it.

My brother asked me if I wanted to go see the manmade pond with the Koi.

I told him that we still had two-hundred-and-ninety-six days before we were supposed to go see the Koi since the last time he told me we would go together to see them.

My brother said he wanted to go now if that was okay with me.

It was okay with me.

My bother said he would let me pick out my favorite rock and he would get it out of the manmade pond for me.

I have the best brother in the world.

I was going to pick a blue rock.

Chapter 6
Will

A Tremendous Amount of Normal

Fridays are usually pretty quiet on campus at the university where I study. The parking lot is typically empty by two o'clock, and foot traffic is often pretty light. I never take Noah to see the Koi because I can never guarantee that there won't be loud cars or people near campus. But I wanted to take Noah after school today. He had been so good that I wanted him to see the Koi finally. He was really good about not asking to see the Koi too often, especially since he was preoccupied with counting down the days until we would go. It was a good enough distraction that he didn't focus on the Koi to the point of becoming anxious.

When we pulled into the campus parking lot, there was just a smattering of cars, and everything was relatively quiet. At least, quiet enough so that Noah wouldn't get overstimulated and get anxious. I opened and closed Noah's car door for him so that he wouldn't have to touch the outside handle. He pulled his hood tightly around his face but didn't cinch it like he normally did outside. Just dealing with the sunlight but not much noise made it so that cinching the hood around his face, creating only a tunnel to look out of into the world, wasn't necessary.

"Do you want to walk over the grass or on the pavement, Noah?" I asked.

I was hoping he'd choose the grass. Noah doesn't mind standing on grass, but he doesn't like walking on it. It feels different under the soles of his shoes and stimulates the soles of his feet too much. He says it feels "squeaky." Even if we had to walk around the parking lot to get to the Koi pond, there wasn't a lot of grass next to the pond, so the adventure should prove possible for him.

"I want to walk on the pavement."

"Okay." I smiled. "Let's walk on the pavement."

When I walk with Noah, I walk close enough that I can grab him out of harm's way quickly, but never close enough that I might accidentally bump into him. I definitely want to make sure that our hands don't accidentally swing into each other's. Noah gets anxious if hands touch him, but hands touching hands is ten times worse.

Noah's meltdowns come in stages. Step one is him looking confused and worried about what is going on. Step two is finger touching. Each finger against his thumb in succession. Then he starts rocking. Then, in step three, he might start some type of self-harm in an attempt to distract himself from the thing that is making him anxious. This involves scratching or hitting his chest or hitting himself on the side of his head with his wrists. Step four is a red alert. This is where an intervention has to be made. If not, he will bang his head against something until there are bruises, scratches, and blood. And he doesn't stop until his Anxiety lessens. Noah knocking himself out might be the only way that it ends if no one stops him.

A missing orange will move him from step one to step four within two to three minutes.

A hand touching his hand takes him straight to step three.

You have ten to fifteen seconds to intervene when he starts off at step three.

And I'm the only person I know of who can intervene effectively.

When we got to the Koi pond, I started to doubt myself as I looked at the six feet of grass between the pavement and the pond. Would Noah have a mini-meltdown if he took three steps towards the pond with grass under his feet? I took a deep breath as we stopped on the pavement next to the pond.

"Do you want to go stand next to the pond, Noah?"

Noah took a minute to think.

"I can't see the Koi well."

"You can see them really well if you stand next to the pond."

"Are they big Koi? Will they splash me? Domestic Koi can reach lengths of fifteen inches, but jumbo Koi can grow to thirty-six inches. They can splash me."

"These must be domestic Koi, then," I answered. "Because most of them are a foot long or smaller."

"Okay."

"Do you want to stand by the pond?"

"Yes."

I took the biggest steps I could as Noah watched, seeing that I could cover the distance in three steps or less. Standing by the pond, I waited as Noah stared at the pond from the pavement. A few moments later, he took two big steps so that he could stand next to the pond. When Noah looked down into the Koi pond, he gasped and "clapped," which consisted of slapping his hands towards each other but not quite connecting. This is something that people with intellectual disabilities might be seen doing. But even highly functioning folks with moderate to severe Asperger Syndrome and ASD do this sometimes. It is one of the ways that they adapt. It's clapping without having to feel their hands touching and without having to endure the sharp crack of skin against skin. It's also a way of showing excitement for people who have difficulty expressing certain emotions with facial expressions.

I love it when Noah does it.

"There's a gold colored one, Will!" Noah was ecstatic. "And a black one!"

"The gold colored one is very pretty." I smiled. "I named him Midas."

"Midas!" Noah was over the moon. "Like King Midas!"

"Do you see that grayish-blue one over there?" I pointed at the biggest Koi in the pond.

Noah scanned the pond.

"Yes!"

"He's my favorite," I said. "I named him Noah."

Noah was "clapping" again.

"You gave the biggest one my name! And he's your favorite!" Noah was getting overwhelmed.

Which worried me. Being overwhelmed with any emotion—even happiness—can lead to Anxiety and meltdowns. Noah's Anxiety is perpetually present, but usually, we can keep it at a low level. When it increases, it increases the likelihood of a meltdown.

Some people On The Spectrum do not show emotions like neurotypical people. They have emotions just like neurotypical people—the whole range of emotions. But anything more than a high level of emotion may not show well. They can be sad, but not frowning. They can be happy but not smiling. But when they hit a certain level of a particular emotion, they show it in excess. When Noah starts "clapping" and gasping, it makes me happy to see him at that level of happiness. But it also worries me. There's a thin line between supremely happy and overwhelmed to the point of a meltdown.

Noah was touching his forefinger to his thumb. I watched him closely but also looked around quickly to see where the safest place was to take him to intervene. After he ran through one round of finger touching, though, he stood calmly and stared down at the pond, and his hands went to his sides. I sighed internally, hoping this meant that we had avoided a meltdown.

"Do you see that red one?" Noah pointed.

"I see it."

"I want to name that one Will," Noah said. "He is the nicest one. He's not pushing the other fish or bumping into them."

I smiled. "His name is Will then."

"They're all really pretty," Noah stated.

"They are." I agreed. "I stop and see them as often as I can. Maybe we'll start coming more often if—"

"Hey!"

I jumped as Noah continued staring down into the pond full of Koi. Turning to see where the shout had come from, I was afraid that a groundskeeper or other staff member was going to scream at us to not feed the Koi. Not that we had planned to or anything. Instead of a surly employee of the university, I saw Manny jogging towards us, his backpack bouncing as he came towards us. I smiled, but my stomach was sinking a little.

"Hey," I responded in a lower voice as he approached.

My back was to Noah as I faced Manny, shielding my brother from this person that he did not know at all. Noah wasn't bad with strangers, but strangers didn't know how to interact in a way with Noah that didn't overwhelm him sometimes. If I interacted with Manny and Noah could just stare at the fish, he could block the stranger out and not have his senses overwhelmed.

"I thought that was you." Manny smiled, panting slightly.

"How far did you run?" I teased.

"Just from the parking lot." Manny chuckled. "I need to get more exercise."

"Wouldn't hurt I guess."

"I thought I wouldn't see you until we worked on our project, but then I remembered that I didn't give you my cell phone number in class, so I didn't know how to get in touch with you to see what time and where this pancake restaurant is."

"Oh, shit." I laughed and slapped myself on the forehead.

Manny smiled as he pulled his phone out of his pocket. I gave him my number, which he programmed into his phone. A ding came from my pocket.

"Now you have mine." He smiled widely.

"Good deal." I nodded but didn't reach for my phone. "Is seven o'clock a good time?"

He shrugged. "Sure. I don't work tonight. Got all the time in the world."

"I pull shifts on Saturday and Sunday afternoons at the store." I nodded with understanding. "Friday evenings are usually good for me, too."

Manny was looking over my shoulder as I spoke. I tried my best to draw his attention back to me.

"Who is this?" He smiled. "You're not cheating on me with another project partner, are you?"

I laughed. A little too sharply. Manny looked back at me with a raised eyebrow.

"So…"

I stood there, chewing at my bottom lip.

"Oh!" Manny blushed. "Sorry. Yeah. Um, I get it."

"I'm sorry?"

"You have a boyfriend or whatever. It's cool."

I laughed. "No. Um, no."

Manny frowned and held his hands out in a "who is he then?" gesture.

"This is my brother." I was chewing at my lip again.

"Oh!" Manny smiled widely. "Where's your other brother?"

"Huh?"

"The younger brother who won't eat just any old bread you bring home from the store?" He laughed.

My lip chewing intensified.

"Will," Noah spoke up. "I like that one."

I turned away from Manny and stepped back over to Noah to look at what he was pointing at in the pond. My eyes followed his finger to the side of the pond.

"The blue one?" I asked Noah.

"The blue one on top of all the brown ones."

"That specific blue one, huh?" I chuckled.

"Yes. I want that specific blue one that is on top of the brown ones."

"Okay."

I rolled up my sleeve and got down on my knees while Noah stood there and watched me closely, making sure that I grabbed the right blue rock. Even though I had rolled up my sleeve, I had to shove my arm deep enough into the water that a bit of my sleeve still got wet. But I grabbed the blue rock easily and pulled it out of the water. I stood up and held it for Noah to inspect as water dripped from my arm. I made sure to stand back far enough so that no water would drip on him.

"That one is really pretty." Noah was ecstatic, but his face was blank. "It's prettier than all of the other blue ones I have."

"That's why you had to come pick one out, Noah." I smiled. "I knew you'd be better at picking out rocks than I am."

"You pick out okay rocks," Noah said. "I don't want it until you wash it."

"I'll wash it as soon as we go home," I replied and stuffed the rock into my jeans' pocket.

Noah went back to staring at the Koi.

I turned to Manny as I rolled my sleeve back down, letting my shirt dry my arm as it rolled down over it. Then I wiped my hand against my jeans.

"Oh." Manny gave a look of recognition.

"Oh." I gave a single nod.

Manny and I stared at each other for what felt like forever. How do you tell a potential new friend that your brother is On The Spectrum? That he might say something about his skin color? His hair? He might tell him to not touch him? That he might ask him any number of questions that are offensive to neurotypicals?

"Does…Noah…want to come with us to have pancakes?" Manny asked.

I chewed at my lip. I was going to make my lip bleed like Noah sometimes did.

"Noah?" I asked as I turned to him.

"What?"

"Do you want to go to the pancake restaurant?"

"Is mom cleaning?"

"Maybe," I replied. "But we can go even if she isn't. If you want to."

Another feeling question. These take time.

"I want to go if I can have pancakes and the sausage patties that come frozen in a box and a glass of skim milk."

"You can have all of that." I smiled. "Do you mind if my friend comes with us?"

Noah suddenly looked over, as though he hadn't been aware up until that point that there was another person with us. That was nearly a first for Noah. He rarely gets so distracted by something that other people don't bother him. Highest blessings to the Koi pond.

"This is Maneesh," I said. "Maneesh doesn't like to shake hands either."

I turned to Manny. He nodded at me.

"Nice to meet you, Noah. People call me Manny."

"Your skin is really dark," Noah said.

"It is." Manny smiled.

"We have the same hair color," Noah said.

"Yours is longer," Manny replied. "It's nicer than mine."

"Your hair is okay. But I'm not gay. I appreciate your hair as another human being. Gay men have all different colors and styles of hair. Or no hair. So, you can't tell if someone is gay by looking at their hair."

"That's true."

"Are you Pakistani?"

"Indian," Manny replied.

"Were you born in India?"

"Vermont."

"Were your parents born in India?"

"Yes."

"Why didn't they want to live in India? I've seen pictures of India, and it's really pretty."

"Have you been to Vermont?"

"No."

"It's really pretty there, too."

Noah looked at me. Not in the eyes. He looked at my chest.

"Do I still get to sit in a booth by myself? I don't want anyone's leg touching my leg." Noah asked.

"You won't have to touch anyone if you don't want to, Noah."

"Okay," Noah replied. "I want to go to the pancake restaurant with you and Manny."

"Okay, Noah." I nodded with a smile. "Are you ready to make big steps?"

Noah looked down at the grass. He slowly turned, moving in a way so as to not make the grass "squeak" too much under his feet.

"Yes."

"Do you think we can do it in two big steps?"

"Yes."

And we did. Noah and I took two big steps, and we were back on the pavement. Manny walked over and joined us on the pavement. Noah and I walked beside each other, but not too close, and Manny followed behind. Luckily, he instinctively didn't get too close to Noah, but he didn't trail so far behind that he looked like he wasn't with us.

Noah acted like he normally did.

Manny didn't change Noah's normal.

I liked that.

Chapter 7
Manny

A Tremendous Amount of Normal

Will explained to Noah that the older lady who was our waitress had dyed her hair from gray to brown because she wanted to try something different. Apparently, this was just like how he tried something different each time they came to the pancake restaurant. Will said that neurotypical people like to try different things just to see if they like them so that they don't miss out on something that might be better than the last thing that they tried. Noah said that didn't make sense. Will told him to remember that neurotypical people don't make sense most of the time. Noah agreed and once again twisted up the Rubik's Cube.

We hadn't even ordered any food yet.

We were the only people in the restaurant on a Friday afternoon. Two waitresses were sitting on stools at the counter. They had been talking and laughing loudly when we walked in but lowered their voices when they saw Will and Noah. Both of them waved at Noah. He waved back jerkily and headed towards a booth that I felt was the same booth they always sat in at this restaurant. Will let Noah slide into his side of the booth and get comfortable, and then he slid into the seat across from him until he was against the wall, making sure his legs didn't hit Noah's as he did so. I followed his lead and slid into the booth next to Will, being mindful of my legs.

Then the waitress had shown up to find out what we wanted to drink.

Noah had told her that her hair wasn't gray anymore. She had smiled at him and agreed that it wasn't as she pulled the Rubik's Cube out of her apron. Will explained about changing one's hair color. Noah took the Rubik's Cube from the waitress with the very tips of his fingers. The waitress passed it to him expertly so that her hand didn't touch his. I watched the transaction between Noah and the waitress—whose nametag said "Shirley"—and thought it was the most achingly beautiful thing that I had ever seen.

Will ordered coffee, so I did the same. Shirley asked Noah if he wanted skim milk and he answered with a simple "yes." Will added a "thank you" for Noah, which Shirley smiled at, and then she went to get our drinks for us. This place was a total dive. It was clean—but it obviously hadn't been updated since the late 80s. Everything was an outdated color and style, and everything was faded. Even the menus looked like they were the same ones from the 80s. But it was very peaceful, far from any major roads, and the staff was very mindful that Noah was present.

I listened as Will told me his thoughts for the project, what he had written up and constructed in his own mind as he checked all of the syrup carafes. He wiped the maple syrup one down thoroughly as he spoke. Then he took Noah's silverware and rubbed every piece with a napkin until it was practically shining like it was brand new. Noah focused solely on the Rubik's Cube as Will went through these motions.

I was new to Will and Noah, but I could tell that there was a lot involved in making sure that Noah was taken care of at a level that he needed to function. Will did it without a complaint for himself or an apology to anyone else. And this was normal for Noah. Things would be wiped down, his silverware would not have water spots, and Will would explain the things in a way that Noah could understand if he couldn't figure them out on his own.

Will put a tremendous amount of energy into making Noah's version of normal continue from one moment to the next. I watched his movements and routines as he took care of Noah and did the things that were required from one moment to the next. Not one day to the next. But from one moment to the next. Each moment of his life with Noah, every event, the minutiae, was ruled by Noah's needs. And Will smiled after each moment, especially when Noah was unbothered.

Noah didn't thank Will.

Will didn't ask for thanks.

In this I see God.

It was like my mother's voice in my head. God was working through Will, taking care of his brother who obviously needed an enormous amount of care. Will was a multi-tasker. He told me all of his thoughts and ideas and laid out the details of what he had figured out for the project on his own, but his eyes and hands never stopped moving. He could discuss every minor aspect of the project while he scrubbed silverware clean with a paper napkin. He could follow my thoughts and ideas while he wiped all of the syrup carafes clean.

In the deepest, furthest parts of my mind, I imagined a day in the life of my new friend, his brother, and the tremendous amount of energy put into making things some version of normal. There were images of making sure that everything was clean. Making sure everything was orderly. Making sure that nothing was too noisy or distracting or overwhelming. Making sure that Noah was protected from things that were not his version of normal. Inventing new ways of communicating with eyes so that strangers knew that Noah was not like them.

And it was profoundly beautiful.

I liked my new friend.

Very much.

Chapter 8
Will

"Do you want me to put your blue rock here?" I asked Noah as I stood at his bedside after getting him settled into bed.

"Yes."

I set it down on his bedside table next to his alarm clock.

"Did you set your alarm?"

Noah gave an incredulous laugh.

"Tomorrow is Saturday, Will."

"Tomorrow is Saturday."

"You wake me up on Saturdays before we go to the university store, Will."

"I do wake you up on Saturdays, don't I?"

"And Sundays."

"And Sundays, Noah."

"I like my blue rock. It's prettier than any of the others."

"You're better at picking out rocks than I am, Noah. You proved that today."

"We picked it out together," Noah stated. "It was easier to find with the two of us looking for the prettiest rock."

That was the closest thing Noah had ever said to "I like spending time with you" directly to me.

"That's probably why."

"You're the best Will that I know."

"You're the very best Noah," I replied. "Even out of the ones I don't know."

Noah laughed incredulously again.

"Goodnight, Noah." I smiled down at him before heading to his door.

"Will?" Noah stopped me.

"Yes, Noah?" I turned to him in the doorway.

"Do you love me, Will?" He asked blandly.

"Oh, gosh." I sighed. "So much, Noah."

"Do you love me because you're gay and you love men?" He asked.

I couldn't help but laugh.

"Do you like all girls?"

I didn't ask him if he loved girls. Noah doesn't understand "love."

"Definitely not."

"There ya' go." I shrugged.

Noah stared at me.

"Do you love me because I'm your brother and you have to?"

"I love you because you're you, Noah," I responded. "But you are also the best brother I could ever have."

"Is Manny gay?"

"I don't know, Noah."

"Why haven't you asked him?"

"Because I can be his friend whether he is or isn't gay."

"Do you think he is?"

"I hadn't even thought about it, Noah."

"I like that he doesn't talk loud and he doesn't touch me."

"I like that, too."

"I like that he likes pancakes and sausage patties that come frozen in a box, too."

"That was quite a coincidence, wasn't it?"

"Goodnight, Will."

"Goodnight, Noah."

I closed Noah's door until it was open just six inches and headed back downstairs. My mom still wasn't home. But it was Friday night, so I didn't expect to see her until Sunday evening anyway. I didn't know where she went during the weekends, and I didn't really care. Having the house free of my mother and my sister on the weekends made it mine and Noah's own personal paradise. Other than the two of us going to the university for six hours on Saturday and Sunday so that I could put in shifts at the store, we could do whatever we wanted. Without fear that something overwhelming would happen at home.

Manny was still standing in the living room, looking at the bookcases along the wall opposite the stairs. Our backpacks were next to the coffee table where we had left them when we had entered the house. I had gone about getting Noah his bath and washing his hair and putting him to bed. Manny had made himself quiet and disconnected from our personal routine while we did the things we did every night. We weren't able to do real work on the project at the restaurant, save kicking around thoughts and ideas and exchanging information we'd gathered on our own.

We had stayed at the restaurant far longer than Noah and I normally did—but it was quiet, and Noah was distracted after his meal with the Rubik's Cube. When we left, it was dark, and it was time to start getting Noah ready for bed. So, I asked Manny if he would want to come to the house and work more on the project. He had agreed wholeheartedly and followed us to the house in his own car. Now Noah was in bed, and there were no distractions from getting actual work done.

"Noah's in bed." I stated as I entered the living room.

Manny turned and smiled.

"He said that he likes that you speak softly and don't touch him. And that you like pancakes and sausage patties that come frozen in a box."

"Let him know that he is welcome."

Manny understood that was Noah's way of saying "thank you." Or the closest he would get to it.

"Are these your books?" Manny turned back to the bookcases and gestured.

"Most of them." I chewed at my lip as I thought. "Yeah. Probably all of them. My collection has taken over most of the bookshelves in the house. Except for the ones in Noah's room."

"I'm glad to see my people represented." He smiled at me as I joined him at the bookcases.

He tapped the spine of *The Satanic Verses* by Salman Rushdie.

"An iceberg is water striving to be land; a mountain, especially a Himalaya, especially Everest, is land's attempt to metamorphose into sky; it is grounded in flight, the earth mutated—nearly—into air, and become, in the true sense, exalted."

"You memorized that?" He smiled.

"It's my favorite line from a book ever."

"It's a beautiful passage."

"There's nothing I love more than books," I stated. "Besides Noah."

"I can see that. What is visible doesn't need evidence. But there seems to be a tremendous amount for both cases."

"There's also some Bhagat, Lahiri, Singh, Seth, and Pritam in there." I gestured at the books and went to sit down on the couch.

"I saw that."

"Okay." I groaned as I hauled my backpack into my lap and unzipped it. "I've got copious notes here, so I hope you're ready. My initial notes are always a clusterfuck of epic proportions. Until I get all of my thoughts together, that is."

"What is Noah's diagnosis?" Manny asked, ignoring what I said.

"Asperger Syndrome—moderate to severe. ASD, of course, but we say 'Asperger Syndrome' because that was Noah's initial diagnosis and that is what he likes. He also has severe anxiety and gets overwhelmed easily." I answered automatically. "Now doctors just say he's On The Spectrum."

"Aren't we all on some spectrum?" Manny laughed.

"There's a scale or spectrum or chart for us all." I agreed.

"How long has he suffered from it?"

"He doesn't suffer from Asperger Syndrome. He suffers from a world that refuses to conform to his needs. He suffers from neurotypical people who don't take time to try and understand him. He suffers from people who are cruel."

114

"I apologize." Manny bowed his head. "I misspoke."

"Since birth, essentially," I answered as I set my backpack on the floor again. "He was diagnosed when he wasn't speaking by age three and would scream and bash his head against things if people touched him with their hands. I had just turned eight. He started suddenly speaking in full sentences when he was five years old—when he was in kindergarten classes for intellectually disabled children. Then he got moved to a traditional kindergarten class. And he's been more intellectually advanced than most of the kids in his classes ever since."

"He can't have hands touching him—fingertips are the worst. He can't touch certain parts of his own body with his hands for too long, or with too much pressure or it is overstimulating. His chest, back, thighs, and feet are the worst. His pajama pants have to be fleece because the cotton kind feels like sand on his legs. And anytime he wears out his hoodies, I have to buy twelve more—always royal blue—that are identical because he has a meltdown when he gets a new hoodie—and I want to push out the next hoodie meltdown as far as possible. Walking on grass sounds 'squeaky' to him and doesn't understand why neurotypical people want to go to war and kill each other. He has a scar on his forehead and cheek from when he bashed his face on the sidewalk to calm down his Anxiety. I have scraped knuckles from when I stopped him from pounding his head against the table the other morning when we ran out of oranges, and my alcoholic bitch mother gave him a pear instead."

Manny came over and sat down on the couch.

"Kids at school call him a retard—which he doesn't understand because he is not intellectually disabled. He doesn't understand insults, proverbs, sarcasm, dishonesty, hyperbole, cruelty—he doesn't understand why people don't say what they mean and mean what they say. He won't eat any bread except the kind that is brown evenly throughout with thin crust and doesn't crumble when he bites into it. He will never look you in the eyes unless he's in the middle of a meltdown."

Manny was staring at me.

"My mother has told him that she wishes our sister was at home more and that Noah and I weren't here. Noah doesn't get offended because he has his favorite people, too. He doesn't understand that moms are not supposed to have favorite children. When our sister calls him a retard, he thinks she just doesn't know the right words to describe his syndrome."

"Noah wants to see a girl's breasts and have sex because he thinks that sex must feel really good. But he wants the girl to be very clean, not touch him with her hands, and not kiss him. He'll probably never find a neurotypical girl who loves him for who he is, as he is. And he will never understand that either. And he'll never be able to change himself even a fraction so that there's a chance. Most people aren't willing to change themselves to meet him somewhere in the middle. He tells people that they are fat or old or dark skinned or homosexual or disabled. But he doesn't call them ugly—because ugly is subjective. People are not ugly to Noah—no matter how cruel they are to him. They're never worthless because everyone serves some purpose."

"So, Noah doesn't suffer from anything. Noah is not special or weird or abnormal. Noah is filled with a tremendous amount of normal. He is everything that people are supposed to be. While his words may sound cruel to a neurotypical person, he is just stating facts. He does not say that a person is fat and that makes them ugly. They are a person, and they also happen to be fat. He doesn't say that a person is old and that makes them worthless. They are a person who happens to be older than he is. The only thing that isn't normal about Noah is that he gets overwhelmed with everything that

117

neurotypical people have learned to adapt to—loud sounds, bright lights, people who talk too much, casual touches and movements."

"When a politically correct neurotypical person says a fat person is 'chubby' or 'heavyset' or 'plump' or 'overweight,' they do it with an air of superiority, with pity. *Look at that poor fat person. They'd be attractive if they weren't fat. We must feel sorry for them. They'll never be as good as us.* Noah sees that fat person as a person who just happens to be fat. That is the only difference between him and the person he is describing. It's just another descriptor to tell two people apart. One is fat, one is skinny. No more, no less. Noah doesn't understand society's idea of what beauty is."

"I love Noah more than anything. More than myself. Just as he is. But he doesn't understand that and he never will. And he will never love me back. Not in the same way. Not in a way that he understands. He'll never look me in the eyes and tell me that he loves me. That's Noah in a nutshell. That's my normal."

Manny kissed me.

I let him.

For five seconds.

Then I gently pushed him away.

"So, why don't we get to work?" I suggested evenly, reaching for my backpack again.

"I'm so sorry." Manny lowered his head and shook it. "I thought that you were…"

"Gay?"

"Yes." He gave an embarrassed grin. "That was…I'm just sorry."

"I am gay," I replied as I pulled my folder of notes out of my backpack.

"Then…do you not like me?"

I sighed and laid my folder in my lap.

"I am not Noah," I said. "I am neurotypical. I don't always say exactly what I mean."

"What did you mean to say?"

"The moral of Noah's story is that he is truly my normal."

"Right."

"And it will forever be my normal," I said. "When you fall in love with this concept of who you think I am—this noble brother who is the caretaker for his mostly highly functioning brother with Asperger Syndrome—especially so quickly, you're falling in love with a very limited view of what that means, Manny. Today was a really good day. It was probably in the top one percent of good days in the history of Noah. Even though one of Noah's teachers had to keep me from punching a bully at

Noah's school in his face until I could see daylight through his skull. The kid who calls Noah a 'retard' and 'fag' and 'gross.' That's a good day. It's a *great* day."

"Noah will never be different than who he is now. He might learn to adapt to how people use words more so that he understands neurotypical people better. But he will never be able to be touched like a neurotypical person. To be given a regular hug. A casual handshake. To ride the subway and have someone brush against him lightly as they pass in the doorway. To jump into a swimming pool and not freak out. He'll never be able to go to the grocery store or the post office or the dentist or doctor—you don't even want to know what dentist and doctor visits entail—or the movies alone. He can't even go to the movies *with me*. It's too loud, and the popcorn makes his hands feel funny, and the armrests are sticky, and the seat cushions feel weird against his butt and his back. In twenty years, I'll be helping Noah, who will be almost forty-years-old, take a bath in just the right temperature water and wash his hair so that it doesn't stick to his forehead and put on his fleece pajamas so that he doesn't have a meltdown just because he wants to go to sleep."

"Things might be better. He might learn more repetitive motions, coping skills, that make casual touches more tolerable. But he might have a meltdown every day when, in twenty years, he still doesn't know why he can't have a girlfriend or wife or kids or a career like everyone else. His emotional state might degrade to a point that he is constantly anxious about his emotions and why he can't understand them. He'll wonder why he is still getting people screaming 'retard' at him in public. When you fall in love with what you think this is all about— you're falling in love with a fairytale. And most importantly, you're falling in love with a package deal. You'll never possess me like two lovers possess each other. And bit by bit, day after day, month after month, year after year, you will grow to hate me more and more. It'll make you bitter. I'll never be your boyfriend first. I'll be Noah's brother before anything else. Forever. And I will *never* feel sorry or guilty about that. No matter who asks it of me."

"People scream racist stuff at me all the time."

"Do you know why?"

"Because I'm brown."

"Noah doesn't know that he's brown. Do you understand?" I asked.

Manny looked at me for a long time.

"Yes."

"Then let's work on this project." I smiled.

"Love possesses not nor would it ever be possessed, for love is sufficient unto love." Manny smiled.

"And think not you can direct the course of love; for love, if it finds you worthy, directs your course." I countered.

"Gibran." Manny nodded. "I didn't count on you knowing the second part of that quote."

"Book nerd." I cocked an eyebrow. "Remember? And Gibran was Lebanese-American."

Manny laughed and reached for his backpack.

"Just so we're clear." Manny turned and smiled evilly at me. "You do think that I'm fucking hot, right?"

"A regular Shahid Kapoor." I laughed.

Manny's eyes got wide as a huge grin overtook his face.

"Well, if Shahid Kapoor was a few shades darker." Manny laughed with me.

"Okay, okay," I added. "If Shahid Kapoor spent a lot of time in the sun."

"I'll definitely take it." Manny nodded with a wide grin.

I smiled at him and opened the folder.

"I don't think that you're noble, Will."

I looked up at him.

"I think that you do the things you do for Noah—that you've allowed this to be your normal, and you keep allowing this to be your normal—because you love him. Not out of duty." Manny said. "I can imagine that some days you think things—awful things that you would only allow yourself to say in your head—and it kills you a little each time. You probably have wished that Noah was never born. Or that he was someone else's brother. Or that your mom wasn't an 'alcoholic bitch' and would take care of Noah. Or that he could be in an institution. But you know that you're just tired. And you don't mean them. And you love Noah enough to keep adhering to this version of normal. Because it would kill you, even more, to imagine life without Noah. And even if you start thinking those awful thoughts every day, you will keep taking care of Noah. Even though he'll never thank you or say that he loves you. And you'll do it with a smile on your face. That's what I think."

I stared at him for a moment.

"Thank you. You're the best Maneesh I know."

"You're the best Will there ever was." Manny smiled. "And I would very much like to be yours and Noah's friend."

"Noah and I would like that."

"Okay." Manny nodded. "Let's kick this project's ass, then."

Part Two

Chapter 9
Will

A Tremendous Amount of Normal

Christmas is Noah's favorite holiday—mostly because it falls during his favorite season of the year. Winter. Winter is cold. Winter is quiet. Winter is the Earth going to sleep, slumbering and strumming with unused energy, waiting for spring to come so that it can gush forth and bring flowers and green leaves and butterflies and birds—and everything pretty that Noah can stare at for hours in the relative safety of our backyard. When winter comes, spring is just around the corner. Everyone gets a break before a fresh assault of beauty is thrust upon us.

Noah loves Christmas trees and Christmas lights and Christmas music—but only if every other light is off and the music is played quietly. We watch the original, cartoon version of *How the Grinch Stole Christmas* every day in the few weeks leading up to Christmas. Noah really likes Christmas because I don't work or go to school, so during his Christmas break, I can be with him all day. That's my favorite aspect of Christmas vacation, too.

Manny wasn't flying home for Christmas— mostly because his parents were Hindu—but also because he'd be going home at spring break and then when he graduated at the beginning of summer. So, I guess his parents didn't object too much. The good thing was that Noah and I had a friend that we shared who could spend time with us and make things less "Noah and Will" twenty-four-seven. Not that I didn't love spending time with Noah—God knows I do—but it was nice to have another neurotypical person present.

Manny couldn't help me with a lot of Noah's needs, but it was nice to have another set of eyes and ears. Noah was slowly warming up to Manny and would actually hold entire conversations with him when Manny was around. Not that a whole conversation is all that long, but for Noah to ask and answer more than five questions of someone besides myself or Mrs. Hess was huge. I loved the hell out of my new friend for bringing that into Noah's life. Noah wasn't so isolated when Manny was around.

On the second day of mine and Noah's Christmas vacation, Principal Hoffman called and asked me if Noah and I could come to visit his store. So, I promised Noah that we could go to Principal Hoffman's bookstore since we hadn't been there since before school started. It was a Tuesday in the late morning, so I felt it was probably safe to take Noah at that time. Regardless, I phoned Principal Hoffman's store to make sure that it was okay. Just as I suspected, he told me that he would make sure that it was okay if I would tell him a time—and if I didn't, he'd come kick my butt.

I smiled and asked him if ten o'clock was okay.

It was.

So, at ten o'clock on that Tuesday, Noah and I walked into Principal Hoffman's bookstore. The bell clanged over the door, which made Noah jump, but when he looked up and saw the old silver bell on a hook, he gasped and clapped for a second. Noah loves shiny things and he loves the sound of bells if it is soft. Then his attention was on the store. There were shelves and books everywhere, neatly organized. But right in the middle of the store, there was an empty shelf and hundreds of books strewn about. It was chaos. My stomach sank.

"There you two are." Principal Hoffman said loud enough to be heard but not loud enough to startle Noah. "I've been waiting all morning for you."

Noah turned away from the chaos to look at Principal Hoffman. His eyes grew so wide that I thought they'd pop out of his head.

"Principal Hoffman," Noah said. "You're not fat anymore."

"You're right, Noah." Principal Hoffman smiled widely, his arms laced over his much slenderer chest.

"You used to be really fat, and now you're not."

"I've been taking care of myself, Noah." He beamed. "It's very nice of you to notice. You've gotten older since I saw you."

"That was one-hundred-and-ninety-three days ago," Noah said. "I had a birthday in August."

"Then I was right." Principal Hoffman laughed. "Are you taking care of yourself?"

"My brother is," Noah replied.

That was a first. Noah lost interest and turned to look at the empty shelf and the books all over the floor. I was praying that this would not make him have a meltdown.

"Noah." Principal Hoffman came from around the corner, really showing off how much thinner he was. "Since you're here, do you think that you can put those books on the shelf in alphabetical order by author's last name for me? You're much younger than me, and you're very smart."

"That's correct," Noah stated simply and went over to the books.

He stepped carefully, like a lion stalking its prey, making sure that he didn't step on a book or slip as he clenched and unclenched his hands into half-fists at his side. I watched him closely, waiting to see if he would have a meltdown. But Noah began picking up one book at a time, reading the spine, then placing it on the shelf. He'd pick up another book, read the spine, and put it before or after the previous one.

Principal Hoffman was beaming at Noah but then turned to me.

"How are you, Will?" He asked, pulling me into a bear hug.

"I'm okay, sir," I replied. "Thanks for inviting Noah and me."

"I'm just glad the two of you could make it." He pulled out of the hug and grabbed my forearm, pulling me over to the counter. "I have something for you and Noah. It's not much, but you can't come to a bookstore without taking home some books, can you?"

"Sir..."

Mr. Hoffman reached under the counter and came back up with three books in his hands and set them on the counter. The top one was a photography book that had photos of animals and landscapes from Africa. The other was a book with pictures and information about all kinds of rocks. The last book was about people On The Spectrum moving from childhood into adulthood. Obviously, the first two were for Noah. The last one was for me.

"Noah will love the Africa and rocks books," I stated evenly.

"He loves animals, landscapes, and rocks." Principal Hoffman gave a half-smile. "And I think you might find this one to be very helpful."

He tapped the third one without looking down.

"It comes highly recommended from my online educators' group." He said. "It has been very beneficial for parents of and educators who teach people with Asperger Syndrome and those on the spectrum. Your Noah is becoming a man, so maybe you have questions doctors aren't great at answering? And…he is *your* Noah, isn't he?"

I looked up at him and swallowed hard before giving a single nod.

"It's very fortunate that Noah is graduating high school at the same time you are graduating college." He stated evenly. "You'll be able to get a great job, move out of your mother's house. I would imagine that one or even two-bedroom apartments are not that expensive for a bigshot electrical engineer."

I chewed at my lip.

"And what a boon that you were interested in such a lucrative career like electrical engineering." He smiled. "Good money in that—and most companies offer great benefits. Just in case one goes to the doctor a lot. So…the book might be helpful."

"Yes, sir." I gave a single nod. "How much do I owe you?"

"Why would I charge you when Noah is doing all of this work for me?" He scoffed. "That would be double dipping, Will."

"Noah really misses having you as his principal," I stated simply.

"Oh, I miss all of my kids." Principal Hoffman sighed fondly, then leaned in. "But Noah was always my favorite. I miss seeing him at lunchtime. You young men need to come and see me more often. I always have shelves that need organizing and stocking. And I sure miss all of my kids. Well, the good ones anyway."

We laughed.

"Okay. But you can't give Noah…or me…free books every time."

"Free?" He scoffed. "I think we've already established that they are not free, Will. I'm offended."

I just smiled at him. Principal Hoffman returned my smile as he looked at me for a few moments, and then he leaned on the counter, coming closer.

"You'll be starting your last semester next month, won't you?"

"Yessir."

He nodded. "It must be quite a burden."

"I'm sorry?"

"Graduating. Getting a job. Leaving the safety of the only home you've ever known. Supporting yourself. More than you already do, that is."

"I suppose."

"Jeez." He reached up to run a hand through his hair. "I remember that time. And I just had me to think of, Will. I didn't have the missus back then to keep me organized and in line. I was such a wreck. I don't know how I made it. Funny thing is—I didn't have the…responsibilities that you do. And I don't know that I would have been able to handle even half of what you may be thinking your future will be like. Hell, I wouldn't have been able to handle a tenth of what you've handled so far. No one would blame you if you decided that your future can't take on anything that would make it more burdensome."

"That's never crossed my mind."

"Of course, it has." Principal Hoffman scoffed. "But, unlike a lot of people—myself included—you'd never even consider it."

I chewed at my lip.

"But no one would blame you if you did." He reiterated.

"I would rather die—because I would anyway." I looked down.

"What a blessing and a curse at the same time."

"Sir?"

"To know what one's life will be in five, ten, twenty years." He stated. "You've been given a crystal ball, Will. But there're two images there, aren't there?"

"I. Would. Die."

"I believe you." He nodded.

We stared at each other for a very long time. On one hand, it touched me that Principal Hoffman told me that no one would blame me for having my awful thoughts. On the other hand, I wanted to hit him for making me think about how much an alternate future would destroy my heart. Changing my future would be easy—but it would absolutely destroy me. I would be able to live with myself…but my heart would be gone.

Noah was my normal.

Noah was my heart.

A Tremendous Amount of Normal

Chapter 10

Manny

"Do you like being in the backseat, Noah?" I asked, looking over my shoulder.

"It's okay."

"If you want to sit up here, just tell me."

"I'm okay here."

Will was chewing at his lip, looking in the rearview mirror of my car.

In the last few months, Will and Noah had let me be their friend, going with them places, eating pancakes with them, playing video games with them, joining in on their daily routines and activities. Will usually drove his car, and Noah sat in the front seat with him while I sat in the back. Noah couldn't sit in the backseat because Will's car was two-door and too many things would touch Noah on the way into the car, and his legs would constantly be touching the back of the front seat also.

For tonight's festivities, I brought my car and asked Noah if he wanted to ride in the backseat of my car. He walked around the car, never touching it, peering in the windows at the backseat. After several minutes, he said that riding in the backseat would be "okay." So, I opened the door behind the passenger seat and let him get inside. I got in the front passenger seat and moved the seat as far up as I comfortably could. I asked Will to drive for us.

"Are you sure that you're okay, Noah?" Will asked, still chewing his lip and looking in the mirror.

"I'm okay," Noah responded.

Will just sat there, gripping the steering wheel tightly, his knuckles white. This was a significant change for both of them. But the person who was on the spectrum was handling it much better than the neurotypical person was. I knew that Will was afraid that Noah would suddenly get anxious or even have a meltdown at any moment. I hadn't witnessed a "Noah meltdown" in the few months that I'd been their friend, but I could tell from Will's daily tension that a meltdown was not something that I wanted to witness if I could avoid it.

But I would.

If I had to.

Anything to help my friends learn to adapt more.

What I felt for Noah. *What I felt for Will.*

I would endure anything.

"Your hair is getting really long," Noah said.

I turned in my seat. "Your hair is getting longer, too."

"Are you gay?" Noah asked.

This topic had not come up with Noah. And I hadn't even talked to Will about it since the night that I had met Noah.

"Yes."

"As a gay man who likes men, do you think that my hair is nice?" Noah asked.

"Your hair is very nice, Noah," I replied. "You're very handsome."

"Do you think that heterosexual girls like my hair?"

Will was getting less tense, his hands gripping the steering wheel a little less tightly.

"I think that a lot of heterosexual girls would like your hair," I responded. "I think some of them would even like you, Noah."

"Do you think my brother's hair is nice?"

"Will's hair is very nice."

"Are you my brother's boyfriend?"

Will was tense again.

"No, Noah. I'm not Will's boyfriend."

"Why not?"

"We're just friends."

"But you like his hair," Noah stated. "And you are both gay and are attracted to other males. Why aren't you his boyfriend?"

"Because we just like being friends," I replied. "We're neurotypical, so we don't understand sex as easily as you do, Noah."

"That's correct," Noah said. "Your hair is okay. Even though I'm not gay."

"Thank you."

"We all have the same hair color," Noah added. "If your skin wasn't so dark, we could be brothers."

Noah meant that people might mistake us all for brothers. Or maybe he meant that he wished we could all be brothers. I was happy with either interpretation.

"I would be very happy to be your brother, Noah." I smiled. "Your brother is very lucky to have you as his brother."

"He is the best Will that I know."

"He's the best Will ever," I said.

Will wasn't gripping the wheel as tightly anymore.

"What color of Christmas light do you like best?" I asked Noah.

"Green and red, obviously." He gave an incredulous laugh. "They're really pretty when there are white lights with them, too."

"I thought blue would be your favorite."

"I like blue a lot," Noah said. "But blue is not a Christmas color. It's okay if there are also blue lights with the green, red, and white lights, though."

"We'll see all of those colors tonight, I'm sure."

Noah didn't respond. Conversation over.

Will's hands were loose on the steering wheel.

"Well, let's go." I turned back around in my seat to look out the windshield. "It's getting dark quickly, and we want to be first in line, right?"

"Yes," Noah said from the backseat.

"Ready?" I asked Will.

"Okay." He chewed at his lip, took a breath, then started the car.

Noah provided a running commentary as we drove through town on our way to see the Christmas lights display that the city put on in the park every year. Lots of other houses had lights and decorations up, and Noah liked to comment that some were "nice" or "pretty" or "really nice" and "really pretty." When we were downtown, he pointed out that a storefront had been decorated for Christmas and that there was a Santa Claus with elves in the front window. Santa Claus wasn't real, though. He found that out when he was six.

It didn't make sense that a fat man could fit down a chimney.

And his house didn't even have a chimney.

And magic isn't real.

And reindeer can't fly.

His brother told him to not tell the other kids at school.

So, he didn't.

But it didn't make sense that they believed in Santa Claus.

I told Noah that I never had Santa Claus when I was growing up since we were Hindu in my family and didn't celebrate Christmas. Noah asked what my family did at Christmas if we didn't celebrate Christmas. I told him that my family didn't really do anything besides eat a lot of my mom's really delicious cooking, but that some Hindus celebrated Pancha Ganapati, which is a relatively new Hindu holiday that is kind of like Christmas. He was really fascinated when I told him that on the second day, a five-headed statue of Ganesha is dressed in royal blue—his favorite color.

On that day, Hindus focus on love and harmony among neighbors, friends, and other loved ones and give gifts—like at Christmas. It's also a day of apologies and forgiveness. Noah asked why people told other people that they liked them and apologized and forgave on just one day. I told Noah that he was very smart to think that. He agreed. I explained this day was for any love, apologies, and forgiveness that people forgot to give the rest of the year. He seemed to understand that.

Then he said he wanted his brother to love him every day.

Will told him that he loved him every second of every day.

Noah laughed.

That was impossible since people sleep for a third of every day.

Will laughed and said that even when he slept, he loved Noah.

He loved Noah so much that he did it even in his sleep.

Noah said he thought that didn't sound correct, but Will was smart, so he probably was right.

My heart was full.

I loved Noah like he was my own brother.

And I was irrevocably in love with Will.

Like he wasn't just my friend.

And that would end up destroying me.

A Tremendous Amount of Normal

Chapter 11

Noah

My brother likes the twinkling lights and the ones that flash really fast.

I like those lights, too.

But sometimes they make me anxious.

I stop looking at them.

My brother gave me his headphones and his MP3 player. It played my favorite song *Porcelain* by the singer Moby really low.

I liked looking at the lights and listening to my song.

Every year my brother takes me to see lights. But he's never taken me to see these lights ever. Manny said that we should all go see the lights and that I should ride in the backseat of his car if I wanted to. Riding in the back of Manny's car is okay. The backseat of Manny's car is really big. It's bigger than the backseat of my brother's car. The seats aren't so hard, and the seat belt doesn't choke me or pull on my body like in my brother's car.

When we got to the really big lights display, Manny told me to put the headphones on and listen to my favorite song. It would make looking at the lights even more fun. He was right. The lights seemed to flash and twinkle like the song does in my head. It was really interesting.

I really like Christmas. It is cold outside, and it snows, and it's really pretty, and I don't have to go to school for 22 days. I like school, but I don't really like all of the noise and really bright lights and the lunch food is not as good as it was when I was in middle school when Principal Hoffman was my principal. Will spends every day with me, and we do really interesting things that I like.

My brother builds snowmen if there's enough snow.

The right kind of snow.

It has to be cold but not too cold so that the snow is a little wet.

My brother lets me sit on the steps of the porch.

And I can watch him build a snowman.

My brother doesn't make me help.

I don't like it when the snow seeps through my gloves and makes my hands wet and clammy and really cold.

I don't like the snow getting stuck in the tread of my shoes.

And my brother understands.

He lets me watch him.

My brother evens lets me decide how he should decorate each snowman. I like it when the snowmen have sticks for arms and a carrot for a nose. My brother will dig out snow to make eyes and a nose for the snowmen so that we don't have to use charcoal. Coal is not good for the environment. Then my brother will let me pick the scarf and hat we put on the snowman. It's really funny when you think about it. Why would a snowman need a scarf and a hat? It's made of snow.

But I like it a lot.

My brother lets me watch *How the Grinch Stole Christmas* every day when I'm not going to school during Christmas.

My brother even watches it with me.

We watch it with the sound off on the T.V.

He turns the lights off in the living room.

And we turn the Christmas tree on.

I don't know what the Grinch sounds like.

Last year, I asked my brother what the Grinch sounds like.

My brother did the Grinch's voice for me.

I really liked that.

Now my brother reads the subtitles on the T.V. for me in the Grinch's voice and in Cindy Lou Who's voice. And he even sings the songs for me.

It's really kind of funny.

I have the best brother in the world.

I don't like that the sound on the T.V. makes me anxious.

I suppose that the voices on T.V. are really interesting.

On Christmas Eve, my brother tells me to take my bath earlier than he usually does. When I'm ready for bed after I have my pajamas on and my hair is washed, we sit in the living room by the Christmas tree and my brother lets me open one gift. But just one. And it is always a new book that my brother found for me. And the book he gives me always has a lot of really interesting writing and a lot of really pretty pictures. Sometimes the book is about rocks. And I really like those. But my favorite book about rocks that my brother got me was about Labradorite. Which is my favorite member of the Feldspar family, mostly because of the labradorescence. Labradorite is composed of aggregate layers that reflect light in colors of blue and green and gold and sometimes red. It's still my favorite book that anyone has ever given me. The Christmas morning after I got the book on Labradorite, my brother gave me another box and told me to open it. It was a really big piece of Labradorite. My brother promised me that I could keep it on my dresser so that I could see it before I went to bed every night and hold it and see all of the reflected colors.

I told my brother that I really liked my gift.

I told my brother that I would hug him, but I didn't want to.

He told me I was the best Noah ever.

Even if I didn't hug him. Because I didn't have to if I didn't want to.

I told him he was the best Will I knew.

Every night for two weeks, before I went to bed, my brother would let me pick up the Labradorite and look at all the labradorescence. And he would ask me which of the colors was my favorite. That was kind of funny. Obviously, the blue was my favorite. But then the rock wasn't there when Will took me to go to bed after getting my hair washed one night. The next morning, when I went to have breakfast, my brother was talking to our mom really loudly.

She said that she hated him.

That she wished I wasn't there and that my sister was instead.

My brother is my favorite person. I wish my mom could be with her favorite person as much as I am with my brother.

My mom called my brother a fag and that she wished he was dead.

When I think about that sometimes, I don't really like my mom.

For a week my brother and I didn't go home after school until it was really late.

We went to the pancake restaurant. I really liked that. The waitresses even let me help them fill up salt and pepper shakers before we went home. But they let me keep my gloves on so that I wouldn't have to feel the salt and pepper on my hands when it sometimes spilled out. That was very interesting.

I don't know why Manny is not my brother's boyfriend.

Manny is okay.

He likes my brother's hair, and he is gay.

Manny would put his hand on my brother's shoulder a lot when we were looking at lights, and I was listening to my favorite song. My brother would look at things Manny pointed out. My brother seemed really happy.

If someone grabbed my shoulder and it made me happy, I would like them a lot.

I think if my brother grabbed my shoulder, I would be okay.

But he doesn't.

Because he's the best brother in the world.

He's the best Will that I know.

Chapter 12
Manny

After the lights display, Will, Noah, and I went to the pancake restaurant. When we first started going to the pancake restaurant together, I held a buried hope that one day we could go somewhere else. Sometime. But, as the months passed, I came to love the pancake restaurant for what it meant to Noah. For what it did for Noah. I even began to love the awful pancakes and bland sausage and horrendous coffee. I found myself craving it. And I'd find myself hoping that Will and Noah would invite me to go to the pancake restaurant every day.

I hoped that Noah would not get tired of sharing Will with me.

I hoped that Will wouldn't get tired of sharing Noah with me.

I hoped a lot of other things that I knew were hoping against hope. And they made my heart long for something that felt like a home that I had never known. Somewhere that my heart knew was home but would never be home. I knew that something else would eventually have to be inserted as a facsimile for something far superior if I wanted to not be utterly destroyed.

And that was the crux of my problem.

Love is a type of total destruction. A beautifully orchestrated abolishment of who a person is. A subjugation of what one is and a metamorphosis into something closer to the truth. Something closer to the most divine aspect of a human being. An apotheosis.

It's impossible for one to wish for love without a willingness to welcome destruction.

I wanted Will to be my destruction.

Everything about Will was anti-destruction. Will's very essence was that of maintaining homeostasis. It was his normal.

But, oh, how I'd let myself be destroyed. I would do it minute after minute, hour after hour, day after day. My moment to moment existence would revel in the destruction that Will could provide.

I yearned for that destruction.

I would allow destruction to be my normal.

I wanted Will and Noah to be my normal.

And that would destroy me.

I welcomed it.

Chapter 13
Will

A Tremendous Amount of Normal

Manny's apartment was very cozy. Small and neat, but lived in. It was a visible reflection of the innermost workings of my friend. Organization and functionality and utility. But there was dust here and there. The hand towel in the bathroom was just askew enough that the sterility of the bathroom was muted. His small bedroom was picked up and orderly, but the wrinkling of the bedspread was temporary proof that he had sat there to tie his shoes that morning. That this was not just a house, but a home, a place wherein the proof that a person existed was found.

The other, smaller bedroom was a comfy office space where Manny did his homework and studying and gaming. Noah stood in front of Manny's computer, staring at the setup that was way more impressive than any we had at our house. When he first saw the computer, he went through a round of touching his fingers to his thumb but calmed down after. Manny let Noah sit in his office chair, which had aluminum arms and a padded seat and back. Noah said that he really liked the chair. Manny told him that he could sit in it anytime that Noah and I came to visit him at his apartment.

"Do you like playing computer games, Noah?" Manny asked as he moved the mouse, bringing the computer to life in the blink of an eye.

"Yes."

"What kinds of computer games do you like?"

Manny brought up a folder of programs and leaned down next to Noah, but made sure that he did not touch Noah or put his mouth close to his ear.

"I like sandbox and RTS games the most."

"Do you like Minecraft?"

"Yes."

"Would you like to help me build up on my Minecraft game?"

"Yes."

Manny turned the volume all of the way down on his computer and opened Minecraft for Noah. Noah waited until the game was open and running and Manny had let go of the mouse and stepped back before he took control of the keyboard and mouse. I stood there, watching Noah appear totally at ease and at home in front of Manny's computer.

"Is it okay if I show Will my books while you play Minecraft?" Manny asked.

"That's okay."

I chewed at my lip as Manny turned to me with a smile. Noah seemed perfectly fine there in Manny's apartment, in his office, playing on his computer. I looked around the room, making sure there was nothing that Noah would be extremely averse to. Manny motioned with his head towards the living room of his apartment. I swallowed down my worry and nodded.

Manny led me into the living room and went directly to the wall of bookcases where most people would have a television. At first, I wanted to ask Manny where his T.V. was, but I figured that, like most people our age, he probably watched T.V. on his computer. No point in owning a T.V. when a computer is essentially the same thing. Manny grabbed me by my shoulders when I stalled and pushed me with a chuckle towards the numerous rows of books.

"I've never been here before," I said stupidly.

"I know," Manny spoke into my ear. "Now I can finally show you my books."

"You have a lot of them."

"You showed me yours." He said. "Now I'll show you mine."

I answered the double entendre with a small smile and moved closer to the books, away from Manny's hands on my shoulders. Like my own book collection, it was evident that Manny had no real system for organizing them. There was no aesthetic reason for his organization, no color coordination, no alphabetizing, nothing. It was just books and

books and books. All shapes, sizes, colors, genres—
it was absolutely beautiful.

"Which one do you think is my favorite?"
Manny asked, overflowing with feigned haughtiness.

I reached out and grabbed the one laying on
its side in front of a row of books.

"This one." I held it out to him. "*The Good
Earth.*"

Manny smiled weirdly.

"Exactly." He took it from me gently, looking
down at it. "How did you know?"

"The way it was laying there. On its side. Easy
to spot. Easy to grab." I smiled. "And the spine
looks like it has spent some time being open."

Manny smiled down at the book in his hands.

"I wanted to kill Wang Lung when he made
O-lan give him the pearls she had stolen from the
rich man's house," I said gently. "When O-lan died,
and Wang Lung finally realized the love he had for
her, I felt bad for him. But not enough that I didn't
still want to punch his face in violently."

Manny looked up at me.

"Kinda made his children wanting to sell off
the land okay, as far as I was concerned." I shrugged.

"Have you read everything?"

I moved further down the shelves and looked
at all of the books.

"I see your people are represented adequately," I answered. "You even have *Mahabharata*."

"White boy pronounced it correctly." He chuckled.

I smiled, my eyes on the books.

"Have you read it?" He asked.

"Never try to do good deeds under the influence of passion, fear, or greed."

"You have, then," Manny replied. "And your meaning is what?"

"I don't see *Ramayana* here." I scanned the shelves. "Nope. It's up there."

"Stop." Manny moved over to me. "Please."

I stopped talking and reached up to run my fingers along the spine of *Slouching Towards Bethlehem.* Manny stepped closer. I was facing the bookshelves, and his chest was so close to my bicep that a single hair might fit between us.

"What do you think my motivation is? What are my good deeds, Will? What is my passion?"

"Please don't," I said gently.

"Don't do what?" He whispered.

"That."

His chest was against my arm. I didn't move away.

"Don't put my body against yours as if it belongs there?" Manny asked lowly. "Like that's where I belong? Like my soul recognizes your soul?"

"*Namaskar.*"

"*I bow to the Divine in you.*" He said.

I turned to face him, my body no longer touching his, but so close that I could feel his warmth. Smell his sweet breath. See the individual strands of hair that comprised the waves of black silk on his head.

"I don't want you to bow to me," I whispered back. "I have nothing to offer for a bow."

"May I stand in front of you with reverence? Or beside you with humility?"

I stared at him.

"Will you allow me to worship the actions derived from your soul and allow my soul to join yours in those actions? May I be so bold as to ask your blessings? May I make you my place of worship? The holy space wherein God places his hand upon my brow and declares me a human being upon whom he has bestowed his favor?"

"Stop."

My body wanted to step away, but Manny's moved the infinity of inches between us and my body decided that it never much cared for infinity.

"May I be so bold as to say out loud my wish for our souls to know those actions together?" He whispered, his breath soft and sweet against my face.

"Depends on which actions you're referring to."

"When the half of a whole acts, the other must follow." He whispered. "And it does so with patience and love, without question or hesitance, because a half is never complete without its other."

"I hate you," I whispered.

"But your soul loves me." He said. "Just as mine loves you."

Manny kissed me.

And I let him.

For five seconds.

Then I kissed him back.

My fingers found their way into that forest of silk upon his head, and his hands found the valley of my back. And our souls bowed to the divine in each other. Manny's hands moved to my face as our mouths parted and he brought my face down to his. His lips found each of my cheeks. My eyelids. My chin. The tip of my nose. He brought my hands up to his mouth. And his lips found the palms, the backs of my hands, and each fingertip. Then his lips gently pressed against mine again.

His breath was soft against my mouth.

"I would take a thousand years of love destroying me if it meant that I could be even a minuscule part of your normal, Will." He spoke against my mouth. "I will let love raze me to the ground every moment of every day. As long as it is yours."

"You are a fool." I sighed.

"You are a fool if you don't want to be the architect of that destruction."

I pressed my forehead against his.

"My future is a grab bag of uncertainties, Manny."

"Let me be the constant, Will." He sighed against my mouth. "Let it be our future. Let my soul complete yours."

I let my lips find his again.

"One milliliter of human saliva can contain up to one-hundred million microbes of bacteria." I heard Noah's voice. "Unclean mouths can contain even more bacteria. I don't want a girl to kiss me like that. Lips feel weird. Lips feel like raw chicken."

I smiled against Manny's mouth, then slowly pulled away.

"Is something wrong, Noah?" I asked, stepping around a smiling Manny.

"I'm thirsty, Will." Noah's forefinger was against his thumb. "I don't like water at other people's houses."

"I know you don't, Noah."

Manny cleared his throat, making sure his smile was gone, then turned to face Noah. He came to stand beside me, his arm touching mine.

"Do you like bottled water, Noah?" He asked.

"I don't like Fiji brand bottled water," Noah said, his hand sliding to his side. "It tastes like minerals and dirt."

"How about Ozarka?" Manny asked.

"I like Ozarka." Noah said. "Ozarka is okay."

"Do you want me to get you a bottle or do you want to get it?" Manny asked. "It's there on the counter in the kitchen. It's not in the fridge."

"I can get it," Noah replied.

So, Noah went over to the kitchen area and took one of the twelve water bottles that Manny had in the corner of the counter.

"I want to play more Minecraft," Noah said simply.

"You can play as much as you want, Noah," Manny replied.

Manny's fingers played against mine as we stood there beside each other and Noah headed back towards the office. In the doorway of the office,

Noah turned, water bottle in hand. He turned to us, his eyes settling on Manny's chest.

"Are you my brother's boyfriend now?" Noah asked.

"Yes," Manny answered quickly before I could say anything.

"Okay."

Then Noah was back in the office.

And Manny was pulling my face down to his again.

Chapter 14
Will

Dr. Mangal entered his office from behind me. I was sat in front of his desk, trying to not strum my fingers against the arm of the chair. Not wanting to look impatient, I was doing my best to look impassive and not too worried. But this doctor's visit was something to be worried about. Mostly because it was the first doctor's visit where I could really be involved in Noah's care and the decisions about his healthcare. Before Noah was eighteen, my mother took care of almost everything having to do with Noah's care. She wouldn't let me get involved. Now that Noah was eighteen, he had a say so in who went to his doctor's appointments with him.

I sat up in the seat, trying not to look too rigid or tense as Dr. Mangal walked around his desk, looking at the folder spread out in his hands. Dr. Mangal was a middle-aged man, hair graying at his temples, round spectacles, a kind face, lithe and lean, appearing as if he could take any person half of his age to the track and beat them. He sat down behind his desk and laid the folder in front of himself. I got tenser as I watched Dr. Mangal read over the data and information in his chart.

The history of Noah.

Noah had never seen Dr. Mangal before in his life. In the last three months of dating Manny, and Manny spending time with both Noah and me, he

175

said he wanted to talk to his parents about Noah. He said that they knew several physicians who might be able to help Noah. I told him that I was okay with that…but I wasn't holding out hope for much. Dr. Mangal came about in his conversations with them. His parents didn't know Dr. Mangal personally, but a friend of a friend of a friend recommended him. They said he was the best child neurologist of which they knew.

Then it became a matter of contacting all of Noah's previous doctors and current doctors. Signing forms. Getting medical records forwarded, making an appointment—all of the fun things that came along with changing an Asperger Syndrome patient to a new doctor. Especially one that had been under spotty care for the first eighteen years of his life. Luckily, when Dr. Mangal found out that Manny's parents had told us to see him, we got an appointment within a week.

"You're Maneesh's boyfriend?" Dr. Mangal looked at me over the top of his glasses.

"Yessir."

I held my breath.

"He could do worse for a boyfriend than a young man who is going to be an electrical engineer. One who cares so deeply for Noah." Dr. Mangal said.

I exhaled slowly. Quietly.

"Have you met Maneesh's parents?"

"Not as of yet." I chewed at my lip. "He wants me to meet them at our graduation ceremony."

He nodded. "I've never met them personally, but friends hold them in very high regard. Dr. Chakrabarti is a well-regarded physician. Mrs. Chakrabarti is a stay at home mother. All of the Chakrabarti children are well liked. Lovely family, so I hear."

I nodded.

"You do know that there are homes for people like Noah, correct?"

"I will walk out of this office." I frowned.

Dr. Mangal studied me.

"I believe you."

"You should." I gritted my teeth.

"May I call you Will?"

"Yes."

"Will," Dr. Mangal took off his glasses and placed them gently on the folder, "it is my understanding that you have been Noah's primary caregiver since he was ten years old."

"That is correct."

"How old would that have made you?"

"Fourteen. Fifteen, maybe."

"I can't imagine." He shook his head and pinched the bridge of his nose.

"What does this have to do with anything?"

"Your brother has severe AS." Dr. Mangal looked me square in the eyes. "And you've managed remarkably. And his AS is severe."

I waited.

"Coming to me this late in his life...I want you to understand some things. You probably are already very aware of what I am about to tell you, but I require that you listen anyway. This may sound harsh, but I would be remiss if we did not discuss these things, regardless of how uncomfortable it can be."

"Yessir."

"Being the primary caregiver for a person with such a severe case of Asperger Syndrome is...it's...most people do not show the fortitude that you have shown. Maneesh's parents have said that, as it has been relayed to them, that you are an extremely patient, loving, and caring guardian—as it were—for your brother. Maneesh is absolutely smitten with you and how much care you have shown your brother."

"I'm not putting him in a..."

He held a hand up.

"That is not what I am suggesting, though I did want to be sure that it was an option if you were not up to continuing to be Noah's caregiver. I want you to be aware that there is no cure for Asperger Syndrome."

"I know that."

"And that we can only help to alleviate symptoms. Such as depression and anxiety. Starting a new routine suddenly so late in life can lead to…"

"Meltdowns?" I cocked an eyebrow. "Self-harm? Sleepless nights? More *coping skills*? Confusion? Loss of functionality? Possibly violence?"

"Yes."

"Been there. Done that. Got the scars to prove it. Both of us."

"I believe that, too." Dr. Mangal put his glasses back on. "From what I can see of you, and your relationship with your Noah…I don't believe that you are confused or misguided in your search for better care for your brother."

"Okay."

"But I want you to know that it is quite possible that it will get worse before it gets better." He leveled me with his eyes. "Much worse, possibly. I do not hand out magic beans or potions. And he may not get better."

"I understand that." I nodded.

"Why is your brother not on an SSRI?" Dr. Mangal asked as he placed his hands atop the open folder, lacing his fingers together.

"Honestly, Dr. Mangal, I have no idea." I pointed at the folder. "I've only been allowed to take over with Noah's medical care when he turned eighteen, so I can only tell you about my experience of taking care of him on a personal level. Everything else you will have to get from that folder."

"Understood." He nodded. "Do you know what an SSRI is?"

"Selective Serotonin Reuptake Inhibitor." I nodded.

"Beyond that?"

"It's often used for depression."

"Correct." He nodded. "I believe, after consulting with Dr. Goldsmith, a developmental pediatrician, and Dr. Patel, a child psychiatrist—both in this practice—that Noah would benefit from an SSRI. Noah is dealing with a considerable amount of depression."

"I don't pretend to understand how depression works in people with AS, Dr. Mangal, but Noah has never said anything about being sad or depressed."

"In AS patients, confusion, and feelings of not understanding people and situations maybe be how depression presents itself, Will." He explained. "Has Noah had a lot of difficulty with these things?"

"Yessir." I nodded. "A lot."

"Noah is incredibly intelligent." He said. "But AS patients do not understand emotions or how to explain their own a lot of the time. At least not like neurotypical people. 'I am confused' or 'I don't understand' may be their way of saying 'I am sad.'"

"I'm following."

"An SSRI will not make Noah finally understand things neurotypical people do or make him never get confused." Dr. Mangal said. "But it will make him deal with these feelings of confusion better and process his thoughts better."

"Okay."

"I see that he was prescribed an SSRI when he was seven years old, but it was never administered or even filled. And it was never mentioned in his records again."

I chewed at my lip and muttered under my breath.

"*Fucking bitch.*"

Dr. Mangal's eyebrows rose. "Your mother."

I nodded and looked down, my eyes watering.

"Yes, well." Dr. Mangal continued. "You are taking care of him now. Let's move forward. If not for your sake, then definitely Noah's. Agreed?"

"Yessir." I looked up, willing my eyes dry. "Absolutely."

"I…we…also believe that a mild sedative, to start with, may also alleviate quite a bit of Noah's problems with anxiety and panic disorder. Anxiety and panic are what make it harder for him to process how he feels and how to more constructively express himself. He is so very anxious that his mind is constantly in a fog." Dr. Mangal said. "Noah tells me that he gets 'really anxious' from a variety of stimuli?"

I nodded.

"That will never change, Will." Dr. Mangal said. "He will always feel sensations at a level that neurotypical people like yourself, and I, will never fully understand. It's like all synapses are firing at once, but not knowing where the target is. It's ping-pong balls bouncing wildly off every wall of his head. A simple touch can overwhelm him to the point that he has to do something, possibly something destructive, to distract himself from the feelings of that stimuli."

"Yessir."

"This is how it is."

I nodded.

"However," Dr. Mangal gave a cautious smile, "I feel that if we can get his anxiety under control...well, it is possible...*possible*...that he will better handle these stimuli that overwhelm him. He will still feel heightened sensations...but the anxiety will be better controlled, so there will not be the level of outward reaction to which you've become accustomed. His AS may seem less severe since he won't be fighting against such a high level of anxiety. He'll always be AS—but maybe we can officially move him to 'moderate' permanently."

I looked up.

"You may never be able to give your brother a *normal* prolonged hug." He sighed, but then looked hopeful. "But maybe a brief one is not out of the question."

Something between a gasp and a laugh caught in my throat. Like a joyous bubble trying to rise in my throat.

"I'm sure you would like that." Dr. Mangal said. "And I am sure that Noah would like that as well."

"I would do anything even for something that small." I breathed out, trying to control my emotions.

"Well," Dr. Mangal stood, so I followed his lead, "I would like you to go speak with your Noah now. I want you to explain to him—in the way that you two do such things—what I've said. Then I want the two of you to make a decision *together* about whether or not we will proceed."

"Noah has shown an interest in girls recently. In sex." I said.

Dr. Mangal sat. He motioned for me to do the same.

"Listen, Will." He took his glasses off again and looked me in the eyes. "We are two grown men, so I'm going to be very blunt with you."

"Please."

"Do you know if your brother has discovered masturbation?"

"No, sir, I don't." I shook my head. "But his trigger zones are his shoulders, upper back, feet, chest, hands, most of his torso, and his thighs—I assume that if he has tried to experiment, it was too overwhelming for him."

"He may be AS, but he is an eighteen-year-old young man." Dr. Mangal and I chuckled. "I'm sure he knows of it at the very least. I think romance and sex is something we leave on the back burner, as it were, until we move forward with any medication therapy."

"What if...what if we move forward?"

"A healthy, sexual and romantic relationship—modified to fit his AS—is not impossible to hope for your brother."

There was nothing to stop me this time. I looked down, and the tears poured from my eyes quietly.

"Okay."

"He may have an adult relationship sometime in his future." He said. "It will never be like what neurotypicals such as you and I would experience...but, it is possible that he may be able to experience these things for himself, in his way, at some point."

"I just want my brother to be happy," I spoke to the floor. "I want him to be as happy as he can be with what he has to work with, Dr. Mangal."

"If we move forward, Will," Dr. Mangal spoke slowly, "and I don't want to give you any false hope...but I believe that if we get Noah under the care he should have been under from the beginning, you will see a relatively quick progression in Noah's overall happiness and development as a healthy, happy human being. He will never understand neurotypical people like other neurotypicals understand them—but he will manage his feelings, confusion, and anxiety about it so much better. It will be overwhelming for both of you. Some of it bad—but a lot of it good. Some of it really bad. Some of it really good. One day, you may forget and lay a hand on your brother's shoulder, and he'll merely flinch…instead of having a meltdown."

I had my hands over my face now.

"How odd to be so happy about something so small." I choked back tears. "To know that my brother might be able to lead something not even close to a normal life."

"What is normal, Will?"

I looked up. "I know what it should be."

"Neurotypical?" He smiled.

"No. To have something like AS—to be locked in its cage—and still want to understand an emotion as extraordinary as love. To want to understand it because you want to make someone else happy. Even when you're not certain of what happy means. To be in your own head yet still be so selfless. That's what it should be."

"In this I see God." Dr. Mangal looked down and muttered.

"Sir?"

"Will," He shook his head with a smile, "I am a man of science. But first and foremost, I am a husband, a father, a son, a brother, a friend, and a soul trapped briefly within a dying bag of cells. Belief sustains us all. And I believe that your brother could not be in better hands."

"I'm sure that you will do your best."

"I'm speaking of you, Will." He stood. "Go speak with your Noah now. Please. I would like to start his medication therapy immediately—if the two of you so decide."

I stood. "Okay.

"I also want you to know that Noah is not a child." Dr. Mangal said. "I am a pediatric neurologist. I am happy to care for Noah for as long as that is appropriate—but in six months, a year, five years...we may need to move Noah into the care of a neurologist who cares for adults."

"But..."

"If I ever tell you that Noah needs to go to another neurologist," Dr. Mangal leveled me with his eyes, "it is because he has progressed so far that he would benefit even more from the care of another doctor. Do you understand?"

I smiled so widely it hurt. "My, God, yes—yessir."

He smiled back. "Then you must speak with your brother."

I started to turn towards the door but stopped myself and turned to Dr. Mangal.

"Sir?" I chewed at my lip. "I don't know what is going to happen. But I just want you to know that this has been the happiest day of my life so far. And, regardless of what happens, I can't thank you enough for that. There's nothing I can do to thank you for that."

Dr. Mangal bowed his head.

"I bow to the divine in you, sir," I said.

"You honor me, Will."

I shook Dr. Mangal's hand and let him lead me from the office and down the hallway to the treatment room where Noah was waiting. Dr. Mangal opened the door to the room but did not enter. Noah was sitting on the exam table, his head inclined to watch the cartoons on the television mounted on the wall. Someone had muted the T.V. and turned on the closed captions for him. Noah was entranced by the program that was on the T.V.

Noah's eyes flitted in my direction for a moment then back to the T.V. I smiled, not letting myself hope too strongly for full cooperation from Noah. And anything else would be a deal-breaker for everything Dr. Mangal and I had discussed in his office. I would never force Noah to do a treatment he didn't want to do. I went over and reached up to hit the power button the T.V. Noah's expression didn't change, but his stare moved from the T.V. to the middle of my chest. I grabbed the stool on wheels that Dr. Mangal had most likely used when examining and speaking with Noah earlier. I pulled it over to in front of Noah and sat down gingerly.

"Noah?" I said. "Did you like Dr. Mangal okay?"

"He was okay."

"You feel okay about what all the things you talked to him about?"

This took Noah a little while longer to process.

"I liked that he didn't touch me a lot," Noah replied. "He let me hold the stethoscope against my chest and back."

"That was very nice of him."

"It was probably very nice."

"I have to talk to you about things Dr. Mangal and I talked about, Noah," I said. "Do you want to talk about that now?"

Noah stared at my chest.

"Yes."

"You know when you get really anxious?" I asked. "When things don't make sense, and you have to touch your fingers to your thumb, and you scratch yourself and hit your chest and sometimes bang your head against things?"

"Yes," Noah replied. "When I get really anxious."

"Right."

"I don't like being anxious."

"I know you don't." I nodded. "And I don't like that you get anxious either. I don't like that you feel anxious, Noah. Dr. Mangal says that there are pills called SSRIs and a sedative that might help you not get really anxious when you can't understand things or get confused or scared."

"An SSRI," Noah stated blandly.

"Do you know what that is?"

"It is for people who get really sad."

"Do you get sad a lot?"

"I get really confused," Noah replied. "I don't understand things, but I know that I should."

"Do you know how that makes you feel?"

Noah stared at my chest.

"No."

"What makes you feel the most confused?"

Noah chewed at his lip and touched his forefinger to his thumb. I braced myself.

"I don't know why people call me a retard. I don't understand when people say things that don't make sense." He said, his finger and thumb separating. "I don't know why people don't like me, Will."

190

"I love you, Noah."

"Because I'm your brother."

"Because you're you, Noah," I said. "Because you're you. But also, because you're the best brother anyone could have. *You're my Noah.*"

"You're the best Will I know," Noah said, his finger going back to his thumb. "Will an SSRI and sedative make me neurotypical? Will the pills make me normal?"

I had to look up so that my eyes wouldn't water. I could lie to myself and everyone else about normal…but, not Noah. He understood things other people didn't. He understood *normal* like no one else did.

"No, Noah." I looked back at him. "Nothing will make you not have Asperger Syndrome. You will always have Asperger Syndrome. You know that, don't you?"

"Yes." Noah did a round of finger touching.

"But, if you want to take the pills Dr. Mangal told me about, the Asperger Syndrome might not make you get really anxious when someone touches you. Or when you touch something or someone. You might not bang your head on things as often. Or at all. You might not scratch yourself or have to use your coping skills and repetitive motions as much or not at all. They might help you have

Asperger Syndrome but not be anxious. Would you like that?"

Noah did one more round of finger touching and stopped, his eyes on my chest still.

"I would like that."

"Noah, if you take these pills, you might get more anxious at first. Things could be really bad before they are good. If you take these pills, you might be very anxious for a while before you start to feel better. We might have to do repetitive motions together a lot. You might not sleep well for a while. Remember when we've stayed up all night doing repetitive motions together and how sleepy you were the next day and how confused you felt the next day?"

I didn't mention to Noah that he might sleep even more. Sleeping more was not a major concern at this juncture.

"Yes."

"That might happen again."

"But it won't be forever?"

"Probably not," I said. "But I can't promise you."

Noah's fingers were touching again.

"So, this is something I want you to decide for us," I said. "I want you to decide for us as brothers what you want to do. You can take the pills, and I will be with you every minute of every day unless we're in school. I will help you when you are anxious or confused or…anything. And if you don't want to take the pills, I'll still be with you forever."

"Will you still love me when I'm really anxious?"

I choked and had to clear my throat.

"Noah, I will love you no matter what you are. Or what you do. Nothing will change that either, Noah."

"Okay."

His hand slowly went back to the exam table.

"Will Manny still be my friend, too? Even if I get really anxious and confused?"

"Manny loves you as much as I do." I smiled. "Manny will still be your friend no matter what happens, Noah."

Noah stared at my chest for a really long time.

"I would like to take the SSRI and sedative." He said.

"Okay, Noah."

Part 3

A Tremendous Amount of Normal

Chapter 15
Noah

I don't like the bus.

The bus driver doesn't keep the air conditioner really cold like my brother does when he picks me up in his car.

And the bus driver doesn't play any good music on his radio when we drive across town.

But the bus driver always says *"Hi, Noah!"* when I get on the bus.

He hasn't known me very long, and I haven't known him for very long. But he's really nice to me when I get on the bus after school. Today is the last day of school, though. So, he won't be picking me up from school anymore after today. I'll still take the bus every day, but it won't be from school. I've only been able to take the bus for two weeks by myself. Will rode with me on the bus for the first two weeks that I rode the bus. Probably because he was afraid I'd get really anxious again. But I do okay. I get anxious, but I don't have to do repetitive motions when I ride the bus. I just have to make sure that I pay attention to the buildings and other cars that pass by. I have to keep my mind occupied, so I don't think too much about the hard, plastic seats and other people who get on and off the bus.

The bus driver lets me sit right behind him every day, so I don't get too anxious and worried. And also so that he can remind me when it's my turn to get off of the bus so that I don't miss my stop. It's not that I don't remember where I am supposed to get off of the bus, but sometimes I get so worried about not getting anxious that I forget to pay attention to where the bus is stopping. So, it's really nice that the bus driver tells me it's time to get off the bus. Even if it's on a day that I remember to look up when the bus stops.

The bus driver's name is Joe. I like him.

He brings me peppermint candies that feel like ice cubes on my tongue and cheeks. I really like those. Sometimes they make me a little anxious, but they taste so good that I usually forget about being anxious. But he only lets me have one because Will told him that I shouldn't have a lot of things that stimulate me, like sugar. Sometimes, though, he'll give me a second one that I put in my pocket so that I can have it when I first wake up the next day. I told Will because I felt weird not telling him, which, for some reason, made Will happy. So, Will said that he wouldn't say anything to the bus driver. As long as I didn't eat too much sugar.

I told him that I wouldn't.

Manny told me to listen to my brother because it's even more important to stick to my dietary needs with my new medications. And I want to keep feeling better, so Manny is right. Manny and my brother have been boyfriends for one-hundred-and-sixty-seven days. Manny told me that if I told people six months instead of the exact number of days, they would understand better. So, I try to remember. Manny is really smart, so I try to do what he says. Manny is my friend and spends a lot of time with me when my brother can't.

I miss it when my brother isn't around all the time.

But I do like spending time with Manny.

I don't say that much to Will because I don't want him to think that he's not the best brother in the whole world. I want Will to keep loving me even though I'm on my new medication and things are changing. Will says that he'll love me forever, and he loves me even when he sleeps. I kind of understand that. Sometimes I go to bed thinking about Will and wake up thinking about him, so I think that I was probably thinking about him in my sleep, too. That's probably what Will means. That nothing keeps me out of his mind. I feel that way about Will, too.

Will hasn't had to hug me in one hundred and twenty-seven days. He hasn't had to hug me since I started my medication. If there's anything I miss about not taking my SSRI and my sedative, it's that. I miss Will's hugs. But I don't say anything because he hugs Manny a lot. And Manny needs hugs, so I don't want to take Will's hugs away from him. They touch chests when they hug, so it's not the same, anyway.

Things have changed since I started taking my medication. It was kind of a slow change. But now things are almost completely different. I like it. But I sometimes miss the way things used to be. Will says that I don't need him with me all day long anymore. And I should be happy about that. I am. I really am. I promise. I think. But…if I could feel this way and also be with Will all day, that would be really nice. I miss not having him pick me up after school.

At least Joe is nice.

But Will says that this is our "new normal."

I kind of know what that means.

I take the bus now.

Will comes home at night.

He sits in the hallway outside of the bathroom when I get my shower at night.

He talks to me as I wash my body, keeping my face and hair away from the water.

Then he talks loudly to me as I wash my hair and face really quickly and shove my hair off of my forehead.

He tells me about his day when I'm drying off and blow drying my hair. And then he sits on the side of my bed once I'm in bed and I tell him about my day. Will asks me questions about what happened at school and then after school when I took the bus, and he laughs at some things I say. And I kind of understand a little. It's my favorite time of day.

Will tells me that our "new normal" is going to change again. Now that he has a full-time job, he doesn't want to stay at home anymore. Our mom is hardly ever home, so it's usually just us anyway. So, I don't know why he doesn't want to be in our house anymore. I don't tell Will that I don't want him to leave, but I want him to be happy, too. I think that that would be really nice.

I want Will to feel normal. But Will leaving does make me really anxious.

Not as anxious as before my medication.

But it's the worst Anxiety I feel now that I'm on my medication.

Chapter 16
Will

A Tremendous Amount of Normal

Manny picked me up from work, a smile on his face. I chewed at my lip, but I was smiling as he took a step upwards to kiss me as I came down the stairs outside of my building. I ran my fingers through that inky silk on his head and told him that I loved him, and he was my favorite Maneesh ever. He kissed me on the tip of my nose and reminded me that he was the only Maneesh that I knew. I told him that he was arguing semantics and should just learn to take a compliment.

You are my normal.

That's what he tells me. And it feels better than "I love you."

Though he tells me that a lot, too.

It feels weird getting into a car after work and not having Noah with me. But after a month, I'm getting a lot better at it, though I miss Noah being around all of the time. It's also weird to be getting off so early in the day, but I'm definitely okay with that. There was something that I really wanted to do, and there's no day like a Friday afternoon to do it. So, Manny drove me home so that I could get my car. Of course, we had to spend a few minutes kissing in the car and telling each other how much we love each other. Because that's also our new normal.

Once Manny and I were able to pull ourselves apart, I got in my car and waved "goodbye" to him. For the moment. It wouldn't be long until we saw each other again. Not long at all. Manny drove off, and I started up my car and headed across town. Noah was waiting on me—whether he knew it or not. I found myself smiling and playing music loudly with the windows down as I made the ten-mile trip to where Noah was waiting for his day to end.

I pulled up to the public library and parked out front in a one-hour parking zone since that would be plenty of time. My steps up the stone walkway were almost a skip, jaunty at the least. I smiled as I stepped through the sliding glass doors into the front lobby and approached the receptionist at the front desk. When I asked her where Noah was, she smiled widely since she's so fond of him, and pointed me towards the fiction section. When I made my way across the large building to the fiction section, I spotted Noah down one of the aisles, a teenager was standing in front of Noah.

I stood back to hide at the corner of the shelf and watched.

"I'm looking for this book for my Introduction to American Literature course, but I can't remember who wrote it." The teenager said. Noah was staring at the teenager's chest.

"What is the book called?"

"It's *As I Lay Dying.*" The teenager said.

Noah chewed at his lip for a second.

"William Faulkner," Noah replied simply. "In the F's down there."

He pointed behind himself.

"Hey, thanks, man!" The teenager smiled widely and dashed away, hoping to get any copy on hand.

I smiled to myself as Noah reached into his cart and grabbed a book to shelve. Principal Hoffman was right. Noah knew about books. He's good at his job. I watched my younger brother, who used to only eat one kind of bread—and now will eat three different kinds, even if he will still only eat purple grape jelly without grape pieces—and I am so happy. The happiness isn't for me. It's for him. I'm happy for his new normal.

Finally, I stepped out from behind the shelf and stepped into the aisle, walking towards him with a smile. Noah shelved his final book, then noticed me walking towards him. Something like a smile appeared on his face, and his eyes got wide. I smiled back and approached him.

"Will," He said.

"Hey, buddy."

"Buddy."

Noah laughed.

Because it's funny.

Obviously, that's funny.

But he didn't tell me that that is not his name.

"Where's Manny?" He asked as his eyes glanced at my chin briefly before going back to my chest.

"He's at his apartment, Noah," I said.

"What are you doing here?" Noah asked.

"I'm here to pick you up."

"I'm supposed to take the bus home."

"Well, I thought today that we'd do something different," I said. "If that's okay with you?"

Noah stared at my chest and that almost smile appeared on his face again.

"That's okay, Will."

"I'm very glad that it's okay with you, Noah."

"What are we going to do?"

"Well, go tell Mrs. Robinson that you're leaving, and then I'll show you," I said. "Don't forget to grab your hoodie out of your locker."

"Okay, Will."

Noah walked away towards the office of the library administrator—who Principal Hoffman asked to give Noah a job. The wonderful woman that immediately said "yes" a month ago when he asked.

The absolutely beautiful woman who spent three weeks helping Noah learn his new job without a complaint or harsh word. I wanted to kiss her when I saw her sometimes. I went up to the receptionist and talked to her until Noah showed up, his hoodie held in his fist.

"Are you ready?" I asked him.

"Yes."

"Then, let's go." I smiled.

When we got to my car, Noah used his hoodie to cover his hand so that he could open his car door and get into the front passenger seat. Just like he'd learned in his cognitive therapy classes. Every time that I see him do it, I want to drop to my knees and thank God. But I contained my excitement, yet again, and climbed into the driver's seat. Once we were both buckled up, I started the car up, turned on the air conditioner and played Noah's CD. At the volume set on number six. Noah didn't even flinch.

The drive across town was uneventful. And that's the best thing I can say about every day with Noah. The days are uneventful. They're boringly normal. It's something a lot like love.

When I pulled into the parking lot of the university, it was completely empty. Classes are over for the semester. I'm technically, but not quite officially, a graduate. Noah got out of the car without prompting from me, using his hoodie again to separate his hand from the handles. But he did it with no show of Anxiety. I grabbed the paper bag from the back floorboard and got out of the car and walked around to his side.

"Let's go see the Koi," I said to him.

"Oh." Noah gasped.

He was happy.

"We need to make sure that Midas, Noah, and Will are doing okay, right?"

"Right."

"Let's go."

When we got to the edge of the parking lot, I looked at the grass and the pavement. Noah stood there, looking down as well.

"Do you want to walk across the grass or on the pavement, Noah?" I asked him.

Noah's face twisted up in a squinch-like grimace.

"I want to walk across the grass."

"Are you sure?"

"It's quicker."

That was a good enough answer for me.

"Okay."

So, we walked across the grass. Noah's steps were stiff and jerky, but we made our way across the grass to the edge of the Koi pond. Noah gasped once he could see all of the Koi down in the pond at our feet. All of the fish had gotten bigger—not by much—but they were bigger. Noah was still the biggest fish in the pond. Midas was still gold. And Will was still happy doing his own thing, not pushing the other fish around. Even the new white Koi who clearly knew how to share food with the other Koi, the one Noah wanted to name "Manny," was doing well.

"They're all still so pretty, Will!" Noah was over the moon again, but there was no clapping or finger touching or fist clenching.

Just happiness.

"Noah is still my favorite." I pointed at the grayish blue Koi.

"He's still the biggest, too!" Noah said.

"He is." I agreed.

Noah watched the fish, his hoodie held in his fist, and I watched Noah, smiling widely at how happy my brother was. Finally, I remembered the bag and opened it up. I chewed at my lip as I held it up to where Noah could see inside. It took a moment, but he finally noticed the bag and took his eyes away from the Koi to look inside of the bag at the small brown pellets.

"Do you want to feed them, Noah?"

"Yes."

But Noah didn't move.

He stared at the brown paper bag.

At the brown pellets.

Finally, he reached for the bag, and his hand slowly moved towards the brown pellets inside. Noah reached into the bag, and his fingertips touched the pellets and he squealed an amazed squeal and pulled his hand back. I laughed. Noah laughed with me. He rubbed his hand against his chest. My heart wanted to explode.

"Wanna try again?" I asked after a moment.

Noah's face twisted up again, and he shoved his hand roughly into the bag, quickly grabbed a handful of the pellets, and tossed them into the pond. Then he was rubbing his hand against his chest again and laughing sharply. Happily. Ecstatically. My heart swelled so much that I thought that my happiness would cause me to be blown to bits. I watched Noah jiggle with adrenaline and glee.

"Hey!" I turned my head to see a man standing on the pavement. "You boys can't feed those fish!"

It was one of the caretakers for the university.

"Fuck right off, please, sir!" I hollered back and waved him away.

The man frowned at me for a moment as I tried to send him a signal with my eyes. Finally, he rolled his eyes and waved both hands at me dismissively before strolling away. I turned my attention back to the pond. Noah hadn't even bothered to pay attention to the man and me. He was focused on the fish.

"Noah is pretty hungry." I laughed.

"He's really fat." Noah agreed.

"Yeah." I smiled. "He's a fat fish."

"Can I feed them once more?" Noah asked.

"Okay." I looked around. "But just once more."

Then Noah was digging into the bag again, throwing pellets, wiping his hand against his chest and squealing with glee and adrenaline.

And I told God that if this was the closest we could get to normal.

The way things were now.

That would be more than enough for me.

And I would thank him every day for it.

I could love this normal until the day that I died.

As long as Noah was a part of that.

As long as Noah was happy.

Chapter 17

Manny

A Tremendous Amount of Normal

Will let himself and Noah into the apartment when they arrived. I was sitting on the couch reading *The Good Earth*. Again. When they came into the apartment, I laid the book down on the coffee table and stood. Will closed the door and walked over to me, immediately pressing his lips against mine as his fingers ran through my hair. My hands rose to his lower back to hold onto him as we kissed each other.

"Gross," Noah stated simply from his spot by the door.

Will snickered against my mouth, his teeth against my lips. I laughed lightly with him as we finally pulled away from each other.

"Hey," I said as Will turned to look at Noah. "When you kiss a girl, do you want me to tell you that you're gross?"

"We'll see," Noah said simply.

Will's hand grabbed mine and squeezed.

That squeeze told me what my boyfriend—the love of my life—was thinking. Noah didn't say "I don't want a girl to kiss me." He just said, "we'll see." I squeezed Will's hand back and looked up at him before planting a kiss on his shoulder. Noah went to the kitchen and got one of the bottles of water off the counter. When he came back to the living room, he looked down at the hoodie in his hand, as though he was confused, then tentatively draped it over the back of the easy chair. He stared at it for a minute, as if deciding if that was okay.

He must have decided that it was okay because his eyes finally left the hoodie and moved to my chin.

"What are we doing here?" He asked. "On Fridays, we go to the pancake restaurant. Usually later, but that's what we do on Fridays."

Will squeezed my hand again. He looked down at me and slowly let his hand fall from mine. He stepped forward and looked at his brother as he chewed at his lip yet again. I swatted him on the butt, and he stopped. Noah flinched at the sound but didn't touch any fingers to his thumb or clench his fist. Another victory. Will looked over his shoulder at me and shook his head with a reprimanding smile.

"Noah," Will said. "I know you know that I don't want to live at home anymore, right?"

"Yes." Noah's eyes suddenly would not stay on anything for longer than a second.

"Manny wants me to move in with him. I want to move in with him, too."

Noah looked at the wall. At the floor. At the couch.

"And he wanted me to show you something," Will said lowly. "Do you want to see it?"

Noah took a very long time to answer as his eyes danced.

"Yes."

"Okay. Come on, Noah." Will motioned with his head.

Will led the three of us into the office. The empty white box that used to be my office. The sight of it made me smile. Noah walked in behind Will, and I brought up the rear. Noah moved to the corner and stood there.

"Where's your computer?" Noah asked, his eyes still dancing.

"It's in my room." I shook my head. "Mine and Will's room."

"Why didn't you leave it in here?" Noah asked.

Will looked over at me. I smiled at him.

"Noah," Will said to his brother. "Manny cleared out the office for you. If you want…"

Will choked.

He looked down at his feet.

He was chewing at his lip.

I knew he was afraid of how Noah might respond.

That the answer wouldn't be what he had wished for.

"Noah." I stepped forward and took Will's hand in mine as he chewed his lip and looked down at the floor. "I emptied out this room because if you want, it would make me very happy if you moved in here, too. This can be your bedroom."

"There's no bed." Noah's eyes were no longer dancing all over.

They were staring at Will's chest.

"Not yet," I replied. "But we thought you might like to bring your bed from the house you live in now. It's nice to have your own bed, right?"

"I like my bed."

"Would you like it if it were here?" I asked. "We would really like it if you moved in here. But only if you want."

Will's grip was so tight that I thought he'd break my hand. I would let him destroy my hand. I had two.

"Do I have to share my room with anyone?"

"No." Will choked out but didn't look up.

I looked at Will for a moment.

"You can have this room all to yourself, Noah." I continued for Will. "It's just your room and no one else's. It's strictly Noah's Room if you want that."

Noah stared at Will's chest.

"Can Will still tell me about his day when I take my shower? Can I still tell Will about my day when I go to bed?" Noah asked. "Will there be bottled water? I don't know if I'll like the tap water here. Water tastes funny at other people's houses."

"This will be your house, too, Noah," I said. "But there will be bottled water if you want it."

"Will we have purple grape jelly without the grape pieces and oranges and skim milk for breakfast?"

"We'll have any food you want, Noah," I said as Will squeezed my hand.

"Okay," Noah said simply. "I want this to be my room."

Will let go of my hand and left the room. I turned my head to look after him, keeping my expression blank for Noah's sake. When I turned my head back to Noah, he was staring at the ground.

"Is Will sad? I don't have to move here. This doesn't have to be my room. I have a room at my house."

"Noah." I smiled. "You know how you used to get really anxious? And you didn't know what to do with those feelings?"

"Yes."

"Will is so very happy that he doesn't know how to handle it," I explained. "He just needs a minute to feel that by himself. But he is very happy. Your brother loves you more than anything."

"Okay."

"Why don't you stay here and think about where you want to put your bed and things while I go check on Will?" I suggested. "Will that be okay?"

"That's okay," Noah said.

I turned to leave and find Will, not that there were a lot of places where he could be hiding in my—*our*—small apartment. But when I got to the door, Noah spoke.

"Will told me that he didn't want to live at our house anymore," Noah said. "I didn't understand that."

I turned to Noah.

"I didn't like that Will wouldn't be there anymore," He said, his eyes on my chin. "I like telling him about my day when I shower and then when he tells me about his day when I get into bed. And I like it when he sits with me at breakfast and when he comes home each day. I didn't like that he didn't want to live with me anymore. It made me feel very confused and anxious. Is that what love feels like to neurotypical people?"

"That's what it feels like for me, Noah," I said gently. "That's how I feel when I'm not with your brother, too."

"Do you love my brother?"

I closed my eyes. "I love your brother so much."

"I like that."

"I like that, too, Noah," I replied. "But your brother didn't want to live in that house anymore. He never didn't want to live with you, Noah. But he was afraid that you might not want to live here."

Noah stared at my chin.

"You can live with us as long as you want, wherever we live. It's not just your brother who loves you. You're my brother now, too. If you want. Do you want that? Do you understand?"

Noah thought for several moments.

"Yes. I want that. But you're still also my friend."

"All brothers are friends, Noah." I smiled. "You can't be brothers without also being friends."

"Okay."

I watched him for a moment.

"I'm going to find Will," I said. "We'll be back in a few minutes, okay?"

"Okay."

Chapter 18
Noah

A Tremendous Amount of Normal

Will says that this is a really big day. He means that it is an important day and a lot of things are going to happen. Will said that if I get too anxious, I just have to put on his headphones and listen to my songs. My favorite song is still *Porcelain* by the singer Moby, but Manny let me listen to a song called *Upward Over the Mountain* by a band called Iron & Wine. I really like that song. Will said that sometime we would look the band up on YouTube together and listen to more of their songs. Because he likes that band, too. I really hope that all of their songs are really good.

I've never worn a suit before. I've never been to a funeral. Or a wedding. Or anywhere that I would have to wear a suit. It makes me a little anxious to think about wearing a suit, but in a good way. I think that girls would think that I look okay in a suit. Manny told me that I'm already so handsome that if I wear a suit, I'll look so handsome that girls will fall in love with me. That makes me anxious, too. Like my stomach has something tickling it. It's kind of nice, I think.

Manny and Will are wearing suits today, too. But they're not wearing their suit jackets like I am supposed to do. They said that there's no point in wearing the suit jackets until later. No one will see them under their graduation robes anyway. I guess that makes sense. Why wear a jacket if you're wearing a robe? It's hot outside today anyway. But I'm going to wear a jacket because I don't get a robe today. I got a robe when Will and Manny took me to my high school graduation. They wore suit jackets that day, but I didn't.

High school graduation was "Noah's Day," Will said.

I guess today is "Will and Manny Day."

My high school graduation was very loud, and a lot of people looked really happy and cheered a lot when people walked across the stage. Will let me wear his headphones the whole time so that the noise wouldn't bother me as much. I had to watch my brother and Manny, though so I would know when it was my turn to walk across the stage to get my high school diploma. Manny told me to pay attention because when my name was called, they would cheer for me and I would know to go up on the stage to get my diploma.

When I saw them cheer, I went up on the stage, and Mrs. Hess was there next to the principal, and she was smiling really big. She handed me my diploma, which was rolled up in a tube. I found out later that it wasn't my real diploma. Will told me that he had already picked up the real diploma at the principal's office before graduation. It's in a picture frame in one of the boxes in my bedroom. Mrs. Hess grabbed my forearm when she gave me the rolled up not-diploma and shook my arm softly. She seemed to be really happy.

It only made me a little anxious when she touched me.

That was really nice. I think.

Will told me that it was nice. And he's really smart, so I know that he is right.

Later that night, Mrs. Hess called on the phone to tell me how proud she was to see me graduate. She told me that I was the best student she ever had and she was very happy that Will and I were doing well. I told her I really liked all of the history classes she taught. That I would miss coming to her class every day because it was the best part of school. Mrs. Hess sounded like she was sad but said that made her so happy to hear me say that. I guess I understand that. She said she is not going to be teaching anymore and she is going to retire. I asked her why and she said she really wanted to spend some time traveling now that she is so old. I told her she is old, but she's not too old.

She laughed and thanked me.

She told me I had to promise to let her know how I was doing since she wasn't going to be seeing me every day at school. I promised.

Principal Hoffman also called to tell me how proud he was that I graduated. He said he had been at my graduation, but I just didn't get to see him that day. He said Will told him we'd come to see him at the bookstore as much as we could. I told him I would like that. Principal Hoffman said he would see me at the library because he comes and volunteers sometimes. But it's usually on the weekends, and I never work on weekends. I spend time with Will and Manny on the weekends. Principal Hoffman said he would just have to volunteer during the week sometimes then. I told him that that would be nice. I told Principal Hoffman that Manny was my new brother. He told me that Manny wasn't my real brother, but maybe my brother-in-law. I told Principal Hoffman I knew that, but I like calling Manny my brother. Principal Hoffman said he was sorry for saying such a thing because I was right. Manny was my brother.

Will and Manny took me to get pancakes after my graduation ceremony. Shirley, the waitress, let me play with the Rubik's Cube again, but she said that one I could take home with me because it was just for me. But she'd still have one for me to play with at the restaurant when I came to see her. She told me my pancakes were free that day since she was so proud of me for graduating high school. I asked her if I could try something different.

Will told me I could try anything and everything I wanted. He said if it wasn't free, he would pay for all of it. Shirley told him to "shut up," and I could have anything I wanted for free. Because I graduated high school. Telling people to "shut up" isn't nice, but Will laughed at Shirley, so I guess maybe I just didn't understand. I asked Will what his favorite thing was and he said it was the chicken and dumplings, so I tried that. I didn't like the dumplings. They felt weird in my mouth. So, I ended up having pancakes and sausage patties that come frozen in the box. But Will said he was proud of me for trying the chicken and dumplings.

I told him that it was his favorite thing, so I wanted to try it because he's the best brother ever.

Will was really quiet then. But Manny said that was really nice of me for wanting my brother to be happy. Manny said he was going to buy us all dessert since it was such a good day. I didn't think I'd like any of the pies the restaurant had, but Manny just let me have extra pancakes instead. It was a good day. I really liked graduating and going to the pancake restaurant with my brothers.

That night Will was really tired, so I told him he didn't have to talk to me while I showered and before I went to bed. Will seemed to get anxious about that, so instead, Manny stood outside of the bathroom and talked about our day while I showered. Then he sat on my bed and told me how proud he was of me and how much he loved being my brother. I told him I really liked that, too. He said he was excited about all of us moving in together.

I told him I would love living in our new apartment.

Manny stopped talking for a very long time. Then he asked me if I knew what I meant. I said I meant that I didn't want to live anywhere if my brothers weren't there. Will is the best brother in the world and Manny is my best new brother and also my really good friend. So, that made me really happy, I think. Because I haven't hardly been anxious at all since I found out that I'd get to live with my brothers for as long as I wanted.

Manny told me his heart was full.

I think he meant he was really happy and didn't know what to do with all of his feelings. I think I feel like that a lot when I'm with my brothers. But it doesn't make me want to do my repetitive motions. Because I don't feel anxious when I am with them.

And I won't feel too anxious wearing a suit.

Chapter 19

Manny

Noah sat on the bed, watching the two of us as Will stood in front of me, looping and knotting the tie around my neck. As Will worked deftly with his fingers, Noah watched intensely. I stared up into my boyfriend's face as he chewed at his lip and worked at the tie knot at my throat, his eyes focusing on the task as intensely as his fingers were. Finally, the tie was knotted to his satisfaction, and he loosened it, then pulled it over my head, being careful to not mess up my own tie or my hair. I stepped away and sat down on the bed next to Noah, making sure to not sit too far away but not too close either.

"You sure you want to try this, Noah?" Will asked. "It's a lot different than the clip-on tie you wore to your graduation."

"Yes." Noah stood tentatively and went to stand in front of Will. "I want to try a real tie."

"Okay." Will stopped chewing at his lip and took a deep breath.

"But take it off of me if it chokes me a lot," Noah said.

"I won't let it choke you, Noah."

I held my breath as Will carefully brought the loop over Noah's head and let it fall loosely around his neck. Using just the very tips of his fingers, Will lifted the collar of Noah's shirt so that it was standing up. Noah was rigid but stayed standing in front of his brother. Will slowly pulled at the tie to tighten it until the knot was against Noah's neck, but not tightly. Then he used just the very tips of his fingers again to turn down the flap of Noah's collar.

Will and I both let out the breaths we had been holding as Noah stood before his brother, staring at his chin. Noah didn't move away from his brother, but instead just stood there, as if expecting this process to have more steps. Finally, Will glanced at me nervously, then spoke to Noah.

"Is that okay?"

"It's okay," Noah said. "It's not like the clip-on tie."

"No." Will agreed. "It's a little different, isn't it?"

"Yes."

"Do you want to wear it today?" Will asked. "It's okay if you don't."

"I want to see what it looks like," Noah said.

"Go look in the bathroom mirror." Will nodded.

Noah walked past Will, out of our bedroom. Will looked over at me, chewing at his lip as he stood there rigidly, awaiting the verdict. *Stop it.* I formed the words with my lips before smiling at my boyfriend. Will tried to smile, but it was a line of nerves on his face. Noah seemed to be gone for a very long time. Finally, he returned. The tie was still in place, and he stared at Will's chin.

"I look good." He said.

"You're very handsome, Noah." Will agreed.

"The handsomest," I added.

"Can I take it off if it chokes me?" Noah asked.

"Anytime it starts to make you anxious, you can take it off," Will replied. "Just put it in your pocket, so you don't lose it."

"Okay," Noah said. "So, I look very handsome."

"The handsomest," Will repeated what I had said.

"Am I more handsome than Manny?" Noah asked. "Because his tie looks good, too. You tied his tie really good."

"Are you trying to get me in trouble, Noah?" Will laughed, realized what he had said, and then abruptly stopped.

Noah wouldn't understand.

Noah gave his version of a smile.

"I want to look again." Then he left to go to the bathroom once more.

Maybe he understood a little.

Will turned his head sharply to me with a smile.

"Baby steps, babe." I smiled back. "Baby steps."

Will looked down at his feet, his smile growing as he stood there, reveling in another small, positive event in the history of Noah. I rose from the bed and came to stand in front of the love of my life.

"It's okay if you think that your brother is more handsome than me, today." I bent so that I could look into his eyes.

Will looked up so that I could stop bending.

"These baby steps are nothing short of divine," I said, reaching up to make sure that his tie was perfect. "When God moves his hand, do not pretend to not notice. One is required to pay notice. Don't dismiss divinity when you see it for the sake of my ego. You love me. That will always be more than enough."

"I'm so happy, Manny." He whispered.

"Nothing makes me happier." I moved my face up to his and pressed my lips against his gently.

"I love you," Will spoke against my mouth, his forehead against mine.

"I love you, too."

"You two kiss a lot," Noah said from the doorway.

Will and I laughed but separated, turning to look at Noah. He had put on his suit jacket. He did look very handsome. Maybe there was hope that Noah would one day have his very own kiss from a woman who understood him as we do. A woman who wanted to understand him. Who would treat him the way that he deserved to be treated. Maybe there would be a lot of kisses in Noah's future. If he wanted them. Or not. As long as Noah had Asperger Syndrome, could function highly and was happy, that was more than enough. Kisses optional.

"I like my suit a lot," Noah said. "I think that I look really handsome."

"You do." Will agreed. "You're the handsomest one here, Noah."

Noah didn't say that he agreed. Or that Will was right. He just turned and walked towards the living room. And that was good enough for me. I knew that it was more than enough for Will. It was almost a "thank you."

Chapter 20
Will

Noah stood with me in the parking lot. His tie was still around his neck, but I was holding his suit jacket for him. It had been too hot for him to wear throughout the entire ceremony, so he had given it to Principal Hoffman to keep track of until the ceremony was over. They had to sit in the very back, where no one would sit too close to Noah. And Noah had to wear his headphones through the whole ceremony, but Principal Hoffman had pointed me out on the stage when I walked across the stage, and then when Manny had walked across the stage.

Principal Hoffman said that Noah had gasped and "clapped" when each of us went across the stage to get our fake diplomas rolled up in tubes. After the ceremony, I met Principal Hoffman and Noah outside in the parking lot, far enough away from everyone else's celebrations so that Noah would feel comfortable. Principal Hoffman had pulled me into a huge bear hug and told me how proud he was to see "two of his favorites" graduate in the same year. We had talked a little about my new job, the fact that Noah and I were going to move in with Manny, and how happy we both were.

Noah was asked by Principal Hoffman how he liked his new job, the move, and his new brother. *I'm really happy I think.* That was his response. And it was more than enough for me. Nothing mattered to me like Noah's happiness. Principal Hoffman gently grabbed Noah's forearms and jiggled them softly, like an alternative handshake. He told Noah that he would see him around the library as often as he could and that he expected us to come to see him at the bookstore on the weekends when we had time. Noah said that we would. I nodded along as my brother answered for us.

And then we were alone.

Waiting.

"Are we going to look at the Koi pond, Will?" Noah asked, his eyes squinting slightly from the sun.

"We have to meet Manny's family first, Noah," I said. "But we will see the Koi before we leave."

Noah nodded and stood there.

"Do you know the best part of today, Noah?"

Noah looked at my chin.

"Having you here with me," I said. "That made the day the best it could be. I'm very happy that you came to see me graduate. Thank you for coming to see me graduate."

Noah stared at my chin.

It wasn't my feet.

It wasn't my chest.

It wasn't just to the side or above my shoulder.

"Do you think Manny's family will like us?" He asked.

"I think they'll love you," I said.

"I really like having Manny as my brother," Noah said.

"Manny loves being your brother more than anything, Noah." I smiled. "He's so happy that you're coming to live with us."

Noah gave an incredulous laugh.

"That's so silly," Noah said.

"What's silly?" I laughed with him.

"Manny doesn't love being my brother more than anything." Noah laughed more. "He loves you more than anything."

"What did you—"

Suddenly, several voices carried across the parking lot. I turned sharply to see where the noise came from and spotted Manny waving spastically with a goofy smile, a man, woman, and his four brothers in tow. My stomach started to twist up in knots, but both of his parents were smiling, and all of the brothers were too busy rough-housing with each other to pay much attention to anything else. When they were getting closer, Noah took a small step back, and Manny turned to his brothers to tell them all to settle down.

Finally, his entire family approached, and I was left standing there, with an instinct that was screaming at me to step in front of Noah. I didn't. He'd be okay. Noah stood there, looking at the ground, but holding his own. I smiled internally as Manny pulled his father forward to introduce me.

"Will, this is my baba." Manny's smile was so wide that I thought his face would split. "Baba, this is the love of my life, Will."

My heart was full.

I've never been introduced to anyone in such a way.

I held out my hand, and he immediately reached for mine with a smile to match his son's. My stomach was no longer in knots.

"It's an honor to meet you R. Chakrabarti." I bowed my head slightly.

"Somebody has been using Google." He said in perfect English with no hint of an accent.

I blushed. "Maneesh told me that I should use 'R.' instead of 'Dr.,' sir." I shot a look at Manny that was equal parts irritated and amused.

Manny and his brothers laughed loudly.

I ignored them. Noah didn't jump.

"It's an honor, Dr. Chakrabarti."

"I am honored to meet the man who has captured my son's heart." He bowed his head in imitation of me.

We both laughed.

Manny pushed his mother towards us.

"This is my ma," Manny said. "Ma, this is Will."

"Namaste." I bowed and pressed my hands together.

We all laughed again, already knowing that Manny had given me etiquette instructions that were far too formal for his obviously westernized parents and the occasion. His mother laughed almost as loudly as the men in her family and extended her hands. She took my hand in both of hers and shook it warmly.

"You are the young man who is keeping Maneesh from coming home to Vermont." It wasn't accusatory, just a statement. "You are very handsome, Will."

"Not as handsome as your son." I blushed.

"Bah." She said. "He is lucky."

"Thank you," I said, taking a deep breath. "This is my brother. Noah."

Noah was staring at the middle of Dr. Chakrabarti's chest. I had told him that if he felt anxious, to stare at Manny's father or the ground. I didn't want him to stare at Mrs. Chakrabarti's chest and unintentionally insult Manny's parents.

"Noah," I said, "this is Dr. and Mrs. Chakrabarti, Manny's parents."

Noah held his hands together as closely as he could manage. Which was pretty close nowadays.

"Namaste." He said.

"It's nice to meet you, Noah." Dr. Chakrabarti smiled warmly.

"My goodness." Mrs. Chakrabarti was delighted. "He's even more handsome than Will."

"Will is okay," Noah said, now looking at Mrs. Chakrabarti's chin.

No one laughed. Obviously, Manny had given his parents and brothers a few lessons, too. Every culture has its customs.

"Mrs. Chakrabarti is right." I smiled at Noah. "You're more handsome than me."

"Will," Noah said.

I took the hint and moved the attention away from him.

"These guys must be your brothers?" I asked.

Manny pushed the youngest of his brothers at me.

"This is—" He began.

"Deepak." I held out my hand. "It's nice to meet you."

Deepak loved that I knew who he was on sight and beamed up at his brother as he shook my hand.

"Vijay?" I held my hand out to the next youngest.

He shook my hand and beamed at his brother, too. The action was repeated with the next oldest, Rajesh, and then with the oldest of all of them, Sai.

"I guess Maneesh and I are both the ugliest brothers in our families," I said.

Everyone did laugh at this.

"Baba and ma would like to see our apartment, Will," Manny said. "And ma has promised to make us all a feast for you and Noah's upcoming move."

"That sounds wonderful." I smiled.

Of course, I'd have to make something acceptable for Noah—but that was just a minor detail now that our normal had changed.

"Will," Noah said quietly beside me.

I turned to look at him, then remembered my promise.

"Oh." I turned back to Manny and his family. "I promised Noah that we would see the Koi before we left. We can meet you at your apartment."

"Our apartment." Manny placed a hand on my chest.

"Where are the Koi?" Deepak chirped. "Are there any of the blue kind?"

I looked over at Deepak.

"Noah," I said. "Do you want to show Deepak the Koi?"

Noah thought about this for a moment.

"Yes."

"Do you want to go get the bag of food from the car or do you want me to?" I asked him.

"I can do it," Noah answered as if this were the most ridiculous question.

"Okay." I chuckled and pressed the button on the key fob in my pocket. "We'll wait right here for you."

"The car is right there," Noah replied with incredulity again.

I smiled to myself and handed Noah his suit jacket. "Here."

"Okay."

Noah took his jacket from me and headed towards the car, which was twenty feet away from us. I watched him for a moment, then turned my head back to Manny and his family. His mother was beaming at me. Manny touched his forehead to his mother's shoulder with a contented sigh.

"Our son is dating out of his league." Mrs. Chakrabarti said to her husband. "Hopefully this one isn't as smart as his degree implies. Otherwise, he'll make a run for it the first chance he gets."

I blushed and looked down as the Chakrabarti family laughed at Manny's expense. The smile on my boyfriend's face told me that he didn't mind a bit.

Chapter 21

Noah

My room is empty.

I feel...

I feel calm.

Because Will and I are moving to Manny's.

Our mom is not here today. Will and I haven't seen her much in...several months. That's what Manny told me to say so that neurotypical people would understand me better when I talk. But he said it's okay if I know that it's been ninety-seven days. It's okay if I know things that neurotypical people don't know. It's okay if I understand things better than neurotypical people. Other people don't have to understand things the same way to be friends.

But my brothers understand me.

And I understand them.

Even if I don't talk the same way that they do. I think that love might be understanding. Because I never have to explain myself to my brothers. Will understands me all of the time, and Manny tries really hard. I think that's what Manny means when he says that Will loves me more than anything. He makes sure he understands me more than anyone else does. He takes time to talk to me like I like to be talked to, even when he's busy. He doesn't do things to make me anxious on purpose. And he always tells me that I'm the best brother ever. That I'm the best

Noah in the whole world. And he thinks about me even in his sleep.

I really like that.

Maybe that's why I try really hard to always understand Will. Because Will makes me feel like I am neurotypical. Like I'm not on the spectrum. He makes me feel like I'm no different than he is even though we know that I will always have Asperger Syndrome. Even though I know that I'll never be normal in the same way that he is. But my brothers don't care. Because they really like me no matter what I am. Will tells me that we have our own kind of normal. That we don't have to be the same kind of normal as everyone else.

I really like that, too.

If I were neurotypical, I wouldn't understand how I feel about my brothers as well as I do now. Most neurotypical people don't seem to know about understanding. A lot of them are really impatient with me. But not my brother. He's never the reason that I feel anxious. So, moving in with Will and Manny makes me feel calm. Not anxious. I think that I am really happy.

When Will walked into my empty bedroom, he asked me if I wanted to go home now, or if he needed to wait for me a little longer. I told Will that I wanted to go home because I didn't like this room as much as my room at our apartment. Will told me that I was the best Noah in the whole world.

I told Will he was the best Will there will ever be.

That's how Manny told me to explain myself. Because my brother would understand and be really happy. I like it when my brothers are happy.

A Tremendous Amount of Normal

Chapter 22
Will

A Tremendous Amount of Normal

"I think that we may have to throw out some duplicates." Manny laughed as we 'stretcher carried' the last big box of my books into the apartment.

I laughed with him as we let the box of books down on the floor in front of his wall of bookshelves with a resounding "thump." With the space available on the shelves, as they were, maybe one box of my books would have fit. However, we both knew that we had a lot of the same books, and we only needed one copy of each so some could go. I leaned back, stretching my muscles as Manny mimicked my actions. The shower was running, and Noah was cleaning all of the dust off of himself. Not that there had been too much. Once he had reached a level of dirty that was bordering on completely unacceptable, I suggested that he get a shower while Manny and I carried the rest of the boxes into the apartment.

He didn't ask if anyone was going to be outside of the bathroom talking to him.

He just went to get his shower.

"We'll give away your copies." I teased.

"How about you let me give away *your* copies?" Manny swung his hip into mine. "Since you're the best boyfriend ever."

I laughed and wrapped him up in my arms. Manny pretended to struggle against me as we laughed together. Our lips finally found each other's and my fingers slid into the black silk on top of his head. Manny's hands rested against my lower back as he kissed me, the length of his body pressed against mine. The shower stopped, but the kissing didn't. Noah would not be shocked by the sight of the two of us kissing in the living room. Though, he would be shocked if the living room was still strewn with boxes the next morning. Manny and I had some work cut out for us before we could go to sleep. Or, at least, before we could go to bed.

Manny moved his mouth to my jawline and kissed me there, then down my neck to my throat, nibbling and kissing as I grinned happily and let him explore my neck with his lips. I ran my fingers through his soft hair as he moaned happily and lowly against my throat. There was nothing that would make me happier than being in our apartment with both my brother and my boyfriend. My heart was full, and my normal was the best normal ever.

"Will," Noah said from the bathroom doorway.

"Yes, Noah?" I chuckled as Manny nibbled at my neck.

"I can't find the hairdryer," Noah said, concern in his tone. "I don't know which box it is in because I didn't pack it and I'm feeling anxious."

Noah knew to tell me he was anxious when he felt like he couldn't handle all of the feelings that he was feeling. Manny pulled away from me immediately so that I could get to Noah quickly. I made a large step over the box next to my feet and traversed the expanse of the living room to Noah, still standing in the bathroom doorway, a towel around his waist and one around his shoulders, his hair dripping water down his face.

"I'll find the hairdryer, Noah," Manny stated calmly as he started to open boxes.

I grabbed the towel from around Noah's neck and brought it up to his head. I patted his face dry and then began drying his hair with the towel as I looked over my shoulder to Manny. Noah stood there as I spoke over my shoulder to my boyfriend and Noah's new brother.

"I think I wrote on the side of the box that the hairdryer's in, babe," I said to him as calmly as I could, hoping that we could avert a meltdown.

"I'll find it," Manny responded. "It can't be hiding too well."

"Will," Noah said.

"We'll find it, Noah, don't get too anxious," I spoke to Noah, though my head was still turned towards Manny. "Look in that box over there. That big one by the island."

Manny looked over by the kitchen, saw the box I was talking about and dashed over as calmly as possible to pry it open. I kept running the towel through Noah's hair as I watched Manny rip the box open.

"Will," Noah said again.

"We'll find it, Noah, I promise," I said, turning my head back to him.

Noah pulled back gently but jerkily, his head coming out from underneath the towel. His hair was sticking up in every which direction, looking like a mop.

"My hair is okay now." He said, staring at my chin. "I don't feel anxious anymore."

I looked at the towel hanging limply in my hands. Suddenly, what had just happened struck me. Manny came from the kitchen at a brisk pace, the hair dryer in his hand. He was somewhat out of breath. Noah looked from my chin to Manny's as I stared down at the towel, tears forming in my eyes. Manny looked from me to Noah for a minute, then the hand holding the hair dryer slowly lowered to his side.

Noah used his forearm to brush his hair back from his forehead. He stepped around us toward his bedroom. I stared down at the towel held in my hands. My hands had gotten damp through the towel. Manny's eyes moved to the towel. Noah turned in his doorway, still holding the towel closed around his waist.

"You're both really weird sometimes," Noah said.

Then he stepped into his bedroom to find his pajamas.

"Did you just…" Manny said breathlessly.

I nodded, my vision was blurry.

"He…" Manny trailed off, his head turning to look towards Noah's bedroom, the door still open. "You just—did you actually use your hands?"

"Yes."

"*Oh my God.*" Manny brought a hand to his mouth. "And he's okay."

I nodded.

Manny wrapped his arms around me and pulled me roughly against him and joyfully planted a wet kiss on the side of my face. A wet laugh escaped my mouth as Manny kissed me over and over all over my face. I felt utterly ridiculous. But I would be willing to feel ten times more ridiculous every day to feel that happy. Manny finished his kisses to the side of my face with a happy laugh before letting me go. I turned to him and put the towel around his shoulders before pulling him roughly into me, pushing my lips against his once again. Manny's hands found my hair for once as he returned my kiss.

"*Who packed my stuff?*" Noah's voice carried in from his bedroom, bland and calm. "*I can't find anything. You guys don't know how to organize things at all. I should have packed my own stuff because then I would know where things are.*"

I snorted as Manny laughed against my mouth.

"*Will. I can't find my favorite pajamas.*" Noah continued. "*I really like the pajama bottoms with the…*"

"With the cartoons all over them." I interrupted him. "I'm coming, Noah. I'll find them for you. I promise."

"*Yeah. Those are my favorite ones.*" Noah stated blandly. "*Or the ones with the fish all over them are okay, too, I guess. But I can't find anything.*"

Manny and I had to keep ourselves from laughing loudly from how happy we were. He gave me another quick kiss and shoved me in the direction of Noah's bedroom. I ran my hand through his hair and ruffled it as I dashed off towards Noah's bedroom.

"I'm coming, I'm coming," I said with a smile. "You're bossy today, Noah."

"I'm not bossy. Next time let me pack my own things, Will."

Chapter 23

Manny

A Tremendous Amount of Normal

Will was sitting at one of the barstools in the kitchen, a half-eaten Everything bagel, smeared with cream cheese, in front of him. His coffee mug was full, meaning he was on his second cup. That made me smile. He never had a second cup of coffee when we went to the pancake house. This was my favorite part of our weekends together at our apartment. Lazy Saturday mornings where neither of us had to be at work, and we could stay in our pajamas until lunchtime. Or later. That was entirely up to us. Not a schedule. It was my favorite part of our normal.

We had started dozens of Saturdays this way since Will and Noah moved in with me, making us a family. I sat sideways on the sofa in the lotus position, staring over the back of the couch at the man I would love until the day I died. And I couldn't have been happier. He was focusing on the local independent paper spread out next to his breakfast plate. Will was so focused that he didn't know how intensely focused I was on just watching him. I loved just watching Will, watching how he behaved when he thought no one was watching, when he wasn't in survival mode.

He was so beautiful.
And he's Noah's brother.
And my boyfriend.

When I first met Noah, the first time I kissed my boyfriend, Will told me that I would grow to hate him. That I would become bitter that he would always be Noah's brother before he was my boyfriend. I had reason to be concerned. But I wasn't. Will expends a tremendous amount of energy making things as normal as possible for Noah. To be kind to his brother. To be compassionate. To understand. To make him feel as loved as he is every minute of every day. And that well is bottomless. The energy never runs out. Will has never made me feel second-best or less important. He makes me feel like I'm an integral part of his normal.

Like I'm Noah's brother, too.

We're a team. The three of us. And maybe one day, God willing, we'd become four. That was all up to Noah and how well he managed his AS. One day, maybe…*just maybe*…he'd find a girl who loved him as much as we did, but in the way a young heterosexual man wants. No matter what kind of "normal" he was. In the meantime, Will and I were perfectly happy. We were a trio. And our normal was infinite. Our normal felt a lot like love. Because it was.

That's what normal should be.

Will flipped a page in the paper and took a bite of his bagel. He chewed at a rhythm that matched his soul. Quietly, gently, with purpose. Mindful. Always mindful. He sipped at his coffee, his eyes closing as he did so, savoring the warmth and earthiness of the coffee. Noah made a noise in his room, and Will didn't freeze—but he perked up, listening for bad sounds. When none were forthcoming, he hollered out to his brother.

"You about ready, Noah?"

"*Yes,*" Noah stated simply from behind his closed door.

I smiled at my boyfriend a fraction of a second before he spun slowly on his stool and caught my eye.

"What are you looking at, handsome?" He waggled his eyebrows at me.

"My handsomer boyfriend."

"Only in my dreams am I more handsome than you." He smiled.

Noah's door opened, interrupting our attempts to out-compliment each other. Noah had his jeans, sneakers, and a Polo shirt on. His purple hoodie was in his clenched fist. Will stared at me a moment longer, then turned his attention to our brother.

"You ready for Principal Hoffman?" Will asked.

"Are you sure that I look good in purple, Will?" Noah was staring at Will's chin. "Will girls like it?"

"You look very handsome in purple, Noah." Will nodded. "But girls will like you more than the hoodie."

"Okay," Noah said. "I like blue more, though."

"I know," Will said. "You look very handsome in blue, too."

Noah thought about this for a minute.

"No girls liked me when I wore blue." He said. "Maybe they'll like me more in purple."

"You just be you, Noah," Will said. "And the right girl will realize how amazing you are. I promise."

Noah stared at Will's chin.

"Just remember all the things Manny has taught you about talking to girls," Will said. "But, most importantly, just be kind. The rest will come."

"Okay," Noah said. "But if the purple doesn't work, I want to wear my blue hoodie next time."

Will chuckled. "Did you remember your headphones?"

Noah laughed as if this was the most ridiculous thing.

"We're going to be at the library." He replied. "No one is really loud at the library."

"But today is different," Will said, chewing at his lip. "You're helping Principal Hoffman with the book sale and—"

"You'll be fine, Noah." I stopped Will. "If anyone gets really loud, or it's too bright, or if you get anxious or don't understand things, you just tell Principal Hoffman. He'll take care of you."

"Obviously," Noah said, agreeing with me.

Will gave a tight smile.

I could see the resolve settle on his face.

He had to let Noah try this.

And if something went wrong—we'd deal with it.

As a team.

"You're going to have a lot of fun, Noah," Will said finally. "And Principal Hoffman is really excited that you are going to go help him."

"When will he be here?" Noah asked.

As if he had been waiting for his cue, Will's phone dinged from its place on the countertop next to the paper. Will picked it up, looked at the message, took a deep breath, then set his phone down. He turned to Noah.

"He's downstairs waiting on you now, Noah."

Noah had been letting himself out of the apartment each morning and catching his bus to his job at the library. He rode the bus home. He let himself into the apartment each afternoon. From the very first day that we had all moved in together. He didn't need Principal Hoffman to come fetch him or have us walk him downstairs. Will worried for the first part of every day about this, but it got easier as the minutes and hours went by. Sometimes, he'd come to visit me at my building at work to whisper his concerns so that I could calm him down. But, for the most part, he handled it well. He knew that there was nothing to do but let Noah live. And we'd tackle each problem as it came.

"Okay," Noah said as he methodically pulled his hoodie on.

Will turned back to his breakfast and paper.

"Goodbye, Manny," Noah said.

"See you later, Noah," I said.

"Right," Noah said. "I'll see you when I get home later."

"I'll see you later, Will," Noah said as he headed towards the door.

"Okay," Will said as Noah walked past him. "I love you."

Noah stopped halfway to the door. Seemed to have a thought, then walked back to Will. He very quickly pressed his chest against Will's back and reached up and tapped his forearms against Will's upper arms. Then he walked away and left the apartment, closing the door behind himself. Will's body was frozen in time. My heart was full as I sighed happily, never wanting this sudden overwhelming happiness to ever go away.

I stood from the couch and walked into the kitchen, retrieving a bottle of water out of the fridge. The ones on the counter were for Noah. Maybe I'd make myself a bagel and a cup of coffee, too. We had all morning to eat breakfast and be a couple. I walked over to the island, across from Will. He looked up into my eyes, a broad smile on his face. I smiled back.

"Was that enough?"

Will nodded.

"It was more than I've ever allowed myself to hope for." He sighed happily.

"Your brother loves you," I said. "He knows how much you do to make things as normal as possible for him. How much you work to be patient and be kind and understanding. He knows what it means when you say that you love him."

"I know." Will looked down at his plate. "Now."

"He's never not known."

"I know."

Will sat there staring at his plate as I stood across from him, separated by the island.

"Why don't you get in the shower?" I grinned evilly. "And I'll join you in a second. Then we'll get dressed and go have a real breakfast, and then we'll go somewhere really loud and bright—so when Noah comes home later, we can tell him all about it? If he thinks he'll like it, we'll take him some time. With his headphones."

Will started to smile, but it turned into an evil grin.

"I'm giving you two minutes from the moment I start the shower." He waggled his eyebrows.

I winked at him, and he was off and running towards the bathroom.

But, like Noah, he seemed to have a thought. He came back to the island to look at me on the other side.

"Thank you for being part of my normal." He said softly before dashing off towards the bathroom again.

The shower started, and I heard Will stripping off his pajamas. I smiled to myself as I moved Will's plate and mug to the sink. I put my water back in the fridge. And this was the start of a normal day. Half of a bagel was eaten. The better part of two cups of coffee were drunk. A paper sat on the counter, half read. Our brother went to volunteer at the public library book sale. Showers needed to be taken. And the love found in understanding was proven with the slightest of hugs.

A lifetime of understanding was conveyed in the slightest of touches.

And understanding was love.

Maybe that's what normal is supposed to be? Having patience and kindness to understand each other. Taking time to let another human being realize that they are loved. To let a brother know that he will never be alone. That he is wanted. To prove that none of us are ever alone. And *normal* is love.

Will was wrong. He wasn't Noah's brother before all things. He was simply Noah's source of normal. And there's nothing wrong with spreading the normal around. Our new family was great at being normal together. As I pulled my shirt off, heading towards the bathroom with a smile on my face, I silently thanked God for our tremendous amount of normal.

About the Author

Chase Connor currently lives in Des Moines, Iowa with his dog, Rimbaud, and spends his free time writing M/M Romance, LGBTQ YA novellas/novels, LGBTQ Paranormal Romance, as well as general LGBTQ fiction, when he's not busy being enthusiastic about naps and Pad Thai.

Chase can be reached at
chaseconnor@chaseconnor.com
Or on Twitter @ChaseConnor7
He can also be found on Chase Connor Books
https://chaseconnor.com
(New blog posts every Tuesday)

He does his very best to respond to all DMs, emails, and Twitter comments from his reader friends and loves the interaction with them. Chase has several novellas/novels for sale on Amazon (and other sites) in ebook and paperback format.

Most of Chase Connor's catalog can be read for FREE on Kindle Unlimited

A Tremendous Amount of Normal

Printed in Great Britain
by Amazon